SUCKULENCE

JADE ROYAL

OTHER WORKS BY JADE ROYAL

African American Romance

Love is Worth the Sacrifice (Completed Series)

Two Halves of a Broken Heart

How Deep is Your Love? (Completed Series)

Seduced: Her Sweetest Obsession (Completed Series)

Savior and Sycret: A Forbidden Love (Completed Series)

Goodbye Love

Paranormal Romance

Phoenix Pack Beast Series

Saved by a Beast (Phoenix Pack Paranormal Book 1)

Craved by a beast (Phoenix Pack Paranormal Book 2)

Confessions of a beast (Phoenix Pack Paranormal Book 3)

The Heart of a beast (Phoenix Pack Paranormal book 4)

Raised by a Beast (Phoenix Pack: The next Generation book 1)

Becoming a Beast (Phoenix Pack: The next Generation Book 2)

Betrayed by a Beast (Phoenix Pack: The next Generation Book 3)

In love with a Beast (Phoenix Pack: The next Generation Book 4)

Siren Series

Snatching the Soul of a Siren (Completed Series)

The Lost Soul of a Siren

SUCKULENCE

JADE ROYAL

COPYRIGHT

Prologue

CAIRO, 1919.

The sex was hard and fast; combusting with passion and urgency. He was so hard, his length had gone sensitive, sparking pleasure in every stroke. She was tight and wanting, squeezing his dick with everything she had. Sweat rolled down his back as he grinded inside of her, digging her down into the mattress. Her nails pierced his skin as she dragged them across his back, tightening her legs around his waist.

"Bite me," she huffed out.

"You know I can't," he breathed, reaching under her and grabbing handfuls of her supple bottom, allowing himself to dive deeper inside of her.

"Please. I want to spend my life with you. There's only one way for that to happen," she begged, her voice lilting with her raging pleasure.

"It could kill you," he groaned. Her muscles squeezed once more, making his eyes roll to the back of his head. Deep growls erupted from his throat, that savage side of him threatening to burst out in the onslaught of pleasure. He brought her legs up, pressing them over his shoulders as he angled himself to get deeper within her.

"You're so deep," she cried out, her stomach seemingly caving in from the consistent jabs of pleasure coming from the thickness that was his erection, drilling her. He hovered over her, watching her pleasure unfold. His deep chocolate eyes began to burn gold slowly, changing into the color she loved to see in his intense gaze.

"Night. I love you," she felt the words tumbling from her mouth as he slammed into her guts and she erupted, coating him with her pleasure. His eyes sparked, and lit up the dark room with amber light. Her eyes fluttered close as she screamed out passionately, her legs shaking from where they perched over his broad, sexy shoulders.

"Please, I love you," she begged, wrapping her arms around his neck. A growl escaped his throat again. His perfectly whitened and sharp fangs slowly slid from his gums. She slowly turned her head, giving him access to her bare neck.

"What if it goes wrong?" Night whispered, desperately fighting that savage part of him that just wanted to latch his teeth into her flesh and feed.

"It won't go wrong." She smiled at him in that easy way she always did that stole his heart in the first place.

"Release inside me and bite me Night," she huffed out. "So we can be together forever." Night gave in. He couldn't do otherwise when her dark eyes, heavy with arousal gazed up at him with such longing. He lowered his head, licking her neck to prepare for his entry. When he slid his teeth into her soft flesh, her body jerked under him, but she welcomed his bite. The first pull of her blood jolted Night into a rush of pleasure. His hips jerked as he came hard, spilling his seed within her. His throat was warm with her blood, as he continued to drink. Her body slowly became limp, but Night kept drinking. When he felt her life essence drain to its last beat, he released his venom into the bite infusing it with her bloodstream. Even though it was hard for a vampire to go this deep into biting and pull himself off,

Night forced his teeth from her body. He retracted his fangs and licked the bite marks on her neck, his saliva a healing agent.

Breathing deeply, he slowly backed away from her body, pulling his softened penis from her inferno. Her eyes were closed, and her body was riddled with sweat. After a changing bite, one's body went into a phase similar like a coma. She wouldn't wake until her body accepted the changes on a cellular level.

While she slept, Night cleaned her body dutifully. He dressed her in a silk slip, that was stark against her soft chocolate complexion.

"Please come back to me," Night whispered as he pushed her wisps of unruly dark curls from her face. He'd never changed a woman before, especially not for a reason as silly as love. She wasn't his mate, yet still he had been able to acquire deep rooted feelings for her. So deep in fact, he could feel his heart change tempo when she was around. Vampires lived a lifetime. Sometimes you never found your mate. You couldn't count on it most times, so Night just followed his heart.

After watching her for a moment longer, Night went to clean himself up. He showered for a long while, letting the steaming water seep through his pores. He bit back the urges that told him he needed to have more blood when he knew he didn't need it. Bloodlust was the killer of most vampires and if one didn't have control, it was easy to fall into the trap. Gulping down those urges, and steeling his mind, Night finally left the shower. He dressed in slacks and a simple t-shirt. She was still sleeping soundly on his large bed. Scooping her into his arms, he carried her out of his bedroom and down the long hallway.

Entering his parlor, he laid her out on the oak table in front of the floor to ceiling windows. A warmth behind him made Night realize he wasn't alone.

"You finally turned her?" the voice asked.

"She begged me too," Night replied softly.

"It's only right. Besides, if you want to have babies with this woman the only way that would happen is if she's one of us," he said.

"And when are you going to have babies, Blaze?" Night asked his oldest and best friend. Blaze chuckled.

"You know I'm not fit for that life. But you are. You're clan leader for a reason. The sexy ones always want you anyways," Blaze joked.

"Only when they realize you won't give them a chance," Night countered. The two men chuckled softly.

"How long has it been?" Blaze asked, pulling the blanket at the bottom of the table up over her body.

"Not long," Night replied.

"I know the bite is taxing on you. Get a little rest. I will watch her for you," Blaze offered. Night smiled, appreciative of his dear friend. The changing bite didn't just affect the one that had been bitten. The one that had given the bite experienced lethargy as if they were drunk from the amount of blood they had consumed to change the person in the first place.

"You are appreciated Blaze," Night said, nodding, He approached the table, leaning down to kiss her on the cheek softly. She was cold to the touch but he knew that once her body had risen from its coma state, she would warm.

Night retreated back to his bedroom; the bed still ruffled from their hours of lovemaking. He fell into the bed, encompassed in her scent. It lulled him to sleep easily.

He slept so peacefully, her scent filling him and consuming his whole body. When a vampire gave the changing bite, it gave him the control over the person he'd changed. It made it so that person had a leader, had someone to answer to. That's how it was to be a sire. Night could feel her essence stitching to him, attaching to his own soul. In his sleep he smiled, loving that brightness she was already bringing to him. They would be together forever just like she had said they would be.

As he slept peacefully, he felt something sear painfully across his stomach. Night growled but didn't want to wake, feeling too good lost in her scent while he slept. He turned over and grunted, prepared to continue sleeping when the pain seared through him again. This time, his eyes popped open as the pain rocked his whole body. Only then, when his eyes were open did he realize how long he'd been asleep. The sun was slowly beginning to creep through his bedroom window, basking the room in light. Pain crippled him again, making him feel as if he was being torn apart from the inside.

"No, no," he groaned, clutching his stomach. He rolled out of the bed, falling on his ass before he was scrambling to his feet and running towards the parlor. His insides felt like it was set on fire. Night fell at the doorway of the parlor, screaming as he grabbed his stomach. Blaze was leaning over her body that was pale and limp. He was blowing into her mouth and pushing against her chest. Night felt what he knew was their essence's stitching together, rip apart violently. His eyes glowed burnt orange in his pain as his fangs dug into his lips, making him bleed.

Blaze whipped around, his eyes glassy with emotion as he continued to push at her chest. The sun had risen completely, and laying against the table, she should have soaked in the sun and be waking up, changed and complete.

"I'm sorry Night. Her body didn't accept the change," Blaze whispered. He backed away from her body, knowing there was nothing else he could do.

"I told her it could kill her," Night growled, feeling the heat of his amber eyes. another violent rip plowed through him; this time he felt it through his heart. He was breathing heavily on the ground, seeing her body limp, dead, on the table.

"Fight it Night," Blaze ordered, rushing towards his friend. He kneeled down and held Night at the shoulders.

"I know it hurts, but fight. You have to fight it." This was the

cost of trying to change someone who ended up dying. Night was feeling her essence rip from his body, but furthermore, his own soul was being torn in half. If he gave into the pain his humanity would be stripped from him and he'd become nothing more than a rogue vampire, only craving blood and the kill.

"Listen to him," the whisper was right next to his ear. Night fought that red darkness inside him enough to look to his left. There she was. Even in her ghostly form she was radiating and gorgeous in her cocoa complexion. Night bit his lips harder, forcing more pain through his body to distract him from the surging bloodlust through his body trying to take him over.

"I told you this would happen. Why'd you make me do this?" he growled, blood dripping down his chin.

"You've shown me a love like no other. I have no regrets. Death comes to us all eventually but not to worry my love, I'll always be with you. But don't turn into a monster over me. You're not a monster." Her cold lips pressed against his cheek. A lone tear streaked down his cheek. He bit back the carnal urges racing through his system that begged him to feed and kill. His eyes slowly calmed, the burnt amber turning into soft flecks of gold. He was grunting as he stuffed down the deep-rooted urges trying to gargle up from his stomach. Not only was he shoving down the savageness inside of him, he was shoving down his own humanity, his own heart, his own emotions. He would never feel again. Not love. Not anything.

"Keep it up Night, you got it," Blaze urged him, more than sick with worry that his friend would become the raging beast humans had a right to fear.

"Take me from this place," Night growled. He looked at the spirit of his loved one just in time to see her smile at him. Her body on the table burst into soft flames against the heat of the sun. A dead vampire.

NIGHT WAS PHYSICALLY weak for weeks, going on months. Every moment he thought about his beloved, that carnal urge returned, making him want to rip everyone around him to pieces. A vampire could withstand losing part of his soul if it happened once, twice, maybe even a third time depending on how strong the vampire was. But losing part of your soul wasn't easy. Hell, it seemed easier to just give in to the urges, to become the demon they had evolved from being.

Laying alone, in a bed that didn't memorize the scent of his beloved, Night was pebbled with sweat.

Kill. Kill. Drink. Blood. The urges were crippling his mind, racking his body with tremors. Blaze was at his side, sitting on the bed.

"Here." He cut open his own wrist and showed Night his potent blood.

"No," Night growled.

"You need to feed. Despite the urges, you have to feed. You can't ignore it. Please. Drink." His stomach growled, knotting from the amount of blood he needed to survive. Night snatched Blaze's wrist and drank hungrily. The taste of Blaze's blood was strong, but the flavor held the bond between the two men. It reminded Night of who he was, and what Blaze meant to him. They'd shared a blood bond when they were only little boys, running from the torches of humans. Night could taste the bond, and it brought back his humanity. The urges dwindled, the sickening thought of killing evaporated from his mind as he fed his body. He let go of Blaze's wrist, sated.

"I thought it would work," Blaze grinned.

"You always have the answers, my friend," Night whispered, his eyes getting heavy with the after effects of his feeding.

"You may hurt right now my friend, but no matter how long it takes I know you will find a new love that will make your heart whole again. We don't live thousands of years to only fall in love once. Unless that was your true mate. But she wasn't.

There is hope." Night just patted Blaze's hand and sunk deeper into the mattress, sleep coming easily with his full belly.

Behind his closed lids, in the deepest part of his mind, Night saw the beauty of a smile. Her lips were lush, her teeth were white and perfect. But even though she was smiling, joy didn't touch her eyes. They were large, deep pools of smoke that called to him. Why was she smiling but she wasn't happy? The vision felt so real, Night felt like he could reach out and touch her cool beige skin. He just wanted to make her smile a genuine smile. Who was she? Where was she? Her name was a whisper across his mind.

Trinity.

Chapter One

"Now remember, these are the people me and your father work with. I will not tolerate any unruly behavior. And I'm talking to you specifically, Trinity Kayne." Trinity looked at her mother and rolled her eyes.

"Mother. Please. Save the lecture. In fact, you wouldn't have to give it to me if you hadn't dragged me along to this snooty fest in the first place. I can just tell every single one of these people smell their own farts and sigh like it's a perfume fragrance," Trinity replied. Her mother's face went hot with anger. She smoothed out her gown and tried to keep her composure.

"You will not talk like that here. Your father and I have a reputation to keep. And that includes having one of the most sought-after daughters in this whole town."

"This is New Orleans, mother. Not Beverly hills. Get over yourself." Even though Trinity had just said that, she knew that this part of New Orleans cared too much about your lineage and how rich your family was, and gossip traveled liked the damn flu. Everyone was in everyone's business. There were the country club men talking about their wives, the tea time women gossiping about their neighbors and how good their husbands treated them. And then there were people like Trinity, who was gifted with beauty, and brains but saw right through these people. Every rich family in this town had a son that wanted Trinity's hand in marriage. And her parents were going along right with it. She'd fought long and hard to not end up as some rich man's doting wife, but the moment she turned 28, she could hear the whispers. She wasn't married, and she hadn't had any children. Like they were living in the 20th century or something. When were women defined by their husband and how many children they had?

"Listen, Trinity. This is an important night for me and your father. Can you just smile and be the beautiful woman that you are? For us?" her mother asked earnestly. Trinity scoffed but she finally gave in.

"Okay mother, I'll be good. I'll just sit here and drink my champagne like a good little girl now," Trinity smiled a fake smile.

"Good." Her mother nodded and walked off, her long train on her dress sweeping the floor.

"You ought to be lucky you get treated as good as you do," the distain came from her younger sister.

"Tracee, if I could give you all the things mother and father are shoving down my throat. I gladly would. However, it seems I can't break free." Trinity had tried running away once. Her family had too many ties and everyone knew who she was. She barely made it out of Louisiana before she was taken home. Her parents had locked her in her room for months. Trinity realized she couldn't try that again. But then she turned legal age and tried leaving again. This time, it was both her parents who hunted her down. They simply would not leave her alone. As their first child, they had to use Trinity to cement their legacy. If she married into another rich family, they'd be the power families. Almost like the Trumps; if anyone considered that power. Family however did mean something to Trinity, so she bit back her own pride and did what she needed to do. Now, she was cooped up again, at yet another gala, where she had to pretend she wanted to be there. She realized that because she had stayed, she'd created a hole for herself. She hadn't gotten a job, and she didn't have money saved up. Her trust fund was all that was keeping her afloat. And her parents could easily cut that off if she stepped too far out of line.

"Look at all these men here. And you get to have anyone you want. And you just are so ready to ruin mother and father's lives. I should have been born first. You're ungrateful." Trinity just blinked up at her sister. They were only a year a part and Trinity wished all the time that she had come second too. But there was no such luck.

"Sit back and have a sip of something Tracee. Before your ears catch on fire," Trinity rolled her eyes.

Doing what she said she would, Trinity stayed sitting for most of the party. Men came and went, all with their parents at their sides, trying to sell themselves to Trinity. They all wanted her hand in marriage to become one with the Kayne family but Trinity wasn't accepting. Sure, she could pretend to be what her family wanted, but marry a man she didn't want? That's where she drew the line.

"Alright, I can't take it anymore," Trinity groaned. She stood from the large circular table, her sequined mermaid dress almost suffocating her. She liked to dress to show her figure, but sequins were not her style. Too bad for her, her mother just about forced her into it.

"Trinity, where are you off too?" Trinity groaned low in her throat as her father caught her trying to leave. She turned around and smiled at the aging man. Even in his early 60s, his skin was well taken care of, and he still packed on the muscle he'd had when he was in his earlier years. His dark skin was radiant, and it made sense a man like him had scooped up her mother who also was one of a kind. Both of them were the power couple everyone wanted to be.

"Just for another drink, father," she replied, trying to lie.

"Not to worry. The waitstaff will bring you another drink. I wanted you to talk with someone," he said. Trinity swallowed the words she wanted to say and just nodded. With a hand around her waist, he led her across the large hall to where her mother was standing with another family. The tall man next to her mother was chatting easily with her, sipping on his own glass of champagne.

"Here she is," her father introduced. The tall man turned around, his smile wide on his handsome face.

"Trent? Wow, I haven't seen you in years," Trinity gasped.

"I went to study abroad and do some charity work. But it's good to be back home," he replied. His eyes twinkled as he looked her up and down.

"My, my, Trinity. You've become quite the woman. And here I thought when I came back, it would be too late for me and you'd be married. Now, I'm hearing you're still available," he replied.

"Well, you know. A girl has got to be picky. Not everyone is good enough for my family," Trinity said, smiling at her parents. Her father beamed down on her, pride swelling in his features.

"Our young lady here has always been smart about the man she wants. And I can't blame her. Her mother is just as smart," he bragged." Trinity could only smile.

"So, what do you think about our young man," a small woman spoke, her voice high like a canary. Trinity knew she was Trent's mother.

"I did have a thing for Trent in high school. But I was no match for this ladies' man. Who's to say I have a chance now," Trinity lied. She was honestly just trying not to let him down too harshly, but that back fired on her incredibly.

"There is only one lady I want, Trinity. And that is you. I will not lose out on a chance to be with you either. That's why I've asked your parents for permission to have your hand in marriage," Trent said. Trinity was ready to laugh and explain to him that things didn't quite work that way. But then, both her mother and father held their glasses of champagne high.

"And we've accepted! You two will be married within a couple months right in the gardens of the country club. It will be perfect!" her father exclaimed. Trinity's mouth only fell open as Trent wrapped his arms around her waist and pulled her close. Everyone at the party was looking at them, clapping at the announcement. Still with her mouth agape, Trent leaned down and kissed her softly. She realized that he was making his claim to her public. Everyone would expect this marriage. Everyone would know she was off limits. Her parents and his parents would become the stronghold around town and all Trinity could do was stare in horror at the man she was supposed to marry.

Chapter Two

"I CANNOT BELIEVE THIS!" TRINITY EXPLODED THE moment she was home alone with her parents. Trent had whisked her around the entire party for the rest of the night like they were already married. He talked for her, told everyone they planned to have at least three children and a honey moon in Jamaica. Trinity was completely thrown. One, she couldn't hardly say anything to object, and two, she was still in complete shock. When the party ended, Trent gave her a kiss on the lips as if they'd been dating for years. How could everyone pretend that this was normal?

"I can't either! Finally! We're getting you married! Trent's family is just as strong as ours with wealth to match. They have ties all around the city and abroad. We can build our business and gain more clients," her mother said excitedly.

"Forget the business! I'm talking about how easily you supposedly accepted a marriage proposal on my behalf? And now Trent is walking around with me on his arm like we're some happy ass couple excited to get married? I mean, how long have you had this in motion?" Trinity asked.

"Trent's parents reached out to us two months ago. Trent was going to be returning and we thought it was a great match.

He's educated and charitable. That kind of man deserves our daughter, plus his family hails from rich lineage. It works out perfectly," her father replied.

"What about the part that the last man I want to marry is Trent?! In fact, I don't want to marry any of these men. Why won't you understand that?" her father looked at her with a tightened jaw.

"Being part of this family means that you have to follow our traditions," he said sternly.

"I don't know why you're complaining Trinity. You used to sneak out at night on the weekends to go mess around with Trent in high school," Tracee said disdainfully. Both her parents gasped out as if she just revealed that Trinity was secretly killing people at night as a hobby.

"Wait. Trinity are you not a virgin anymore?" her mother asked worriedly.

"Trent asked us specifically if he'd be your first and only and we were adamant that you weren't that kind of woman. Now are you to tell us that you've been sneaking around?" her father questioned. Trinity looked at Tracee with hardened eyes. Her sister was never going to be nothing more than angry and jealous. Trinity had no idea why, especially when it was clear she didn't want the life her parents were forcing onto her.

"I'm 28 ma. Of course I've fucked," Trinity rolled her eyes.

"Trinity! You do not use that language in this house!" her father exploded. Trinity crossed her arms over her chest.

"For your information, I used to sneak out to see Trent, yes. I had a little crush maybe. But then I realized what a jerk he was. Even in high school. I never had sex with him no, but I'm also not the prissy little virgin you make me out to be. I keep telling the both of you this is not my life. I hate it."

"Well too damn bad! You need us. You've got no money, and you can't possibly get a job around these parts. No one will hire you. They know we control this town. And if you leave, you'll have no money to survive. This is the life you've gotta live. Trust me, once you marry Trent you'll be happy. Even if it seems hard now. What you need to do is explain to Trent why you're not a virgin anymore and pray he still wants to marry you," her mother assured her. Trinity shook her head.

"Is that how you had to accept your life Rose Kayne?" Trinity asked her.

"As you can see, I'm a successful and happy woman. You'd do well to listen to me," Rose stated. Even saying that, Trinity saw the lack of emotion in her mother's eyes. She could pretend to be happy all she wanted to, but Trinity saw right through it. Her father wasn't a bad man but James Kayne didn't move like he loved her mother. It was all just an arrangement.

"Whatever," Trinity scoffed. She kicked off her shoes and went to the parlor where her father kept his wet bar. She quickly found a lowball glass and poured herself a shot of rum.

"Be careful now," her father warned. Trinity looked at him as she threw back the shot.

"I'm your daughter. I know how to handle my liquor," she replied.

"I know well what you're capable of. But trust me Trinity, listening to your mother is important. Marry Trent. He's the perfect male to secure a future with. He'll protect you. Keep a solid home. Give you children. Support you. You'll be taken care of."

"What about my happiness, father?" Trinity asked.

"Happiness comes with time," he shrugged.

"Oh, just like for you and mom? Because you two are just so happy," Trinity exclaimed sarcastically. Her father only gave her a sly grin.

"You go and talk to Trent. He needs to know the status of your body," he said.

"Oh my god, this is not the 50s!" Trinity shouted as her father turned and left the parlor. Trinity poured herself another shot before she left the parlor. The house her parents occupied was large, the sign of their wealth. Trinity left the main house and crossed the courtyard lined with seasonal plants, flowers, and small trees. The house was surrounded by tall black gates to keep the public eye away from their property. Behind the gates, the large house was like its own plantation.

Trinity crossed the courtyard to her wing of the house. It was where most of the guest rooms were and Trinity insisted she have a separate part of the house away from her sister and her parents. She couldn't be around them all the damn time. She needed a break. Now, more than ever she needed time to think. Marry Trent? Seriously? He was very handsome and in high school if she was shallow enough she would have fell for his woes, but nothing could make her ignore the fact that he was so damn cocky. It was too much for her. And now as adults he could either be worse, or maybe he was humble now. Still, her parents were right. Because she didn't think about what her future would look like, she hadn't secured any of her own money. She was simply living in the luxury of her own parents and now she was paying the price for that small ounce of vanity she had. Because now, she feared she was truly stuck.

Once in her bedroom, Trinity stripped from the ridiculous dress she had to wear to the event that night and changed into her favorite. Form fitting high waist jeans and a black cropped t-shirt. She threw on a leather vest and looked at herself in the mirror. Her hair was long, down past her shoulders. She crunched up her nose as she stared back at her image. She hated when her hair was straight. But that was part of the act. Straight hair, long dresses, and jewelry. She quickly brushed her hair into a high ponytail. She'd be excited when she washed the straightness away and got her kinky curls back.

After dressing, Trinity left her room, walking through the darkness of her side of the house. She grabbed *cycleworld*, her favorite motorcycle magazine from the desk in her office before she left the house. Instead of alerting everyone to her departure, she left her car and decided to walk. The night was sticky, but it was something she was all too used to. Maybe by the time she returned home, the effects of the flat iron to her head would sweat out and her curls would begin to plump through.

"You should know you can't just sneak out," her mother called out just before Trinity left the gates. Of course she couldn't leave without someone catching her. they had cameras and servants, and one of them were always telling her parents just exactly what Trinity was doing.

"You wanted me to go talk to Trent. I'm going to talk to Trent," Trinity scoffed.

"Dressed like that?" Rose recoiled.

"Women wear jeans now mother. Trust me, Trent will like it. My ass looks pretty good in it," Trinity smiled.

"I don't know what to do with you," Rose shook her head.

"You look like you're going to *that* part of town. The part of town no human would dare enter without caution," she scolded.

"And if I was?" Trinity teased.

"No! Trinity, please don't! I know we don't agree and we have two different outlooks on life, but trust me, you cannot go to that place. It's horrible and dangerous!"

"Mother, I know what it is. I can look out for myself. And besides, I'm only teasing you. I'm not going over there. What insane reason would I have to even get myself aligned with creatures that aren't even human?" Trinity asked. Rose let out a deep breath, her body shaky, proof that she was truly afraid.

"The last time I encountered one of those things Trinity, it nearly killed me." Rose slid her top to the side and showed Trinity the three scar marks on her shoulder.

"I understand, mother. Not to worry. I dress like this because this is who I am. Not because I want to become a vampire. Relax. And my blood wouldn't interest them. They probably think I'm just as snooty as everyone who lives up here," Trinity smiled. She patted her mother on her shoulder and finally left from the confines of that house. She wasn't going to *that* part of town, but she was going somewhere close. Definitely not to see Trent either.

Chapter Three

"Trinity?! Did you walk all the way here?" Emma opened the door to her small home, surprised when she saw Trinity standing there.

"You always ask that when you know I always walk here," Trinity breathed, trying to catch her breath. Emma dragged her into the house and settled Trinity around the kitchen table. She poured out a glass of sweet tea and cut a slice of lemon cake for Trinity.

"Sweet tea and cake, you're my savior," Trinity teased. Image was everything in her part of town, and cake with sweet tea was definitely something her parents would scold her for eating. Trinity had a good figure but she hardly cared about that. She loved food, especially when it was sweet and sticky.

"How was your party?" Emma asked, sitting around the table. Emma lived on the other side of the swamp. The part of town that knew rich snooty people existed in their town and only longed to be part of it. Emma was different. she didn't care about rich folks, she just lived her life. That's what Trinity admired, and that's why they'd been friends since middle school. Emma had the life Trinity wanted. She lived in a medium sized house that was decorated colorfully and always smelled of cooked food and sweets.

"You remember Trent? The little cutie from high school?" Trinity asked.

"The one with all the looks but a bad ass attitude?" Emma smiled.

"Yup. Him. My parents arranged our marriage," Trinity said. Emma's mouth fell.

"Are you fucking serious? They're forcing you to get married to that fucker?" Emma asked.

"Sad thing is, it's not like I can escape from it. I've got no money and they've got ties all around this state and in others."

"You can always come live with me, I told you that. And I'll get you settled until you find a job," Emma offered.

"Remember, I've tried to get a job before. It's like people see my last name and shake with fear then try and kiss my ass. It never fucking works out. And I couldn't stay with you. You're already working hard to make ends meet. I can't be another burden," Trinity shook her head. Emma smiled slowly, a teasing smile that told Trinity the woman had a secret.

"My money problems aren't what they are anymore. I quit my second job and now I work regular hours like every normal person."

"You quit?! What the hell Emma, where are you getting the extra money from?" Trinity asked.

"Bitten," Emma shrugged. Trinity knew well what Bitten was, and was surprised her friend had even gone there.

"Wait. Little shy Emma went to a vampire sex club? The part of town where humans aren't allowed? The part of town where if humans go there, then our laws can't protect us? The part of town where Vampires just roam around at night, just looking to feed off humans? Have you lost your mind?" Trinity gaped. Emma scoffed.

"I didn't think you of all people would be so judgmental," Emma sighed.

"Don't confuse my concern for being judgmental honey. You know I've always wanted to go to vamp town. I'm just fucking afraid. Are you safe going over there?" Trinity asked.

"I'm safe enough Trinity. I promise. But that's why I specifically go to club Bitten. I give them my blood and they pay me for it. And I mean, they really pay." Emma stood from the table, heading toward her bedroom. Trinity snatched up her glass of sweet tea and gobbled down her cake before she followed her best friend. She walked into Emma's bedroom, outfitted with a queen size bed made with a luxurious comforter and new furniture.

"Whoa, you did some serious decorating," Trinity gasped. Emma went into her night table drawer and pulled out an envelope, filled with money. Trinity had seen plenty money before, her parents spent it like water, but seeing Emma with over 5 grand in an envelope gave Trinity shock.

"They paid me five grand to drink my blood. I only had to let two of them feed and I was leaving there with more money than I make in a month! All in one night! I only go on the weekends, so imagine, four weekends in a month, five thousand dollars each time? I can finally move into a bigger house soon. Pay for my mother to have good care in a better nursing home, support the rest of my family. I can even open the yoga center I've dreamed about since high school. All for letting a vampire feed. I don't see any trouble with that," Emma shrugged.

"I mean, hell, of course there's no trouble with it. As long as it's safe. You're not afraid of being turned into one of them?" Trinity asked.

"Honestly, I think my life would have better quality if I was one of them. Rather than dealing with these humans that don't know how to appreciate life." Emma shrugged.

"What's it like?" Trinity asked. "To be bitten. To have your blood sucked?" Emma gave her a wicked smile.

"Honestly Trinity, it's the best feeling in the damn world."

"That's what you said when Germaine from round the way fucked you all damn night for your birthday," Trinity joked. Emma burst out into laughter.

"Germaine's dick is good. That's why I keep him on speed dial. But getting bitten is like ten orgasms all in one. Every time I leave, my panties are soaked through. Last time, I brought my vibrator. That, plus a bite? Girl, I thought I was crippled when it was over. Plus, vampires are sexual savages. He saw me with the vibrator and he took it from me. I thought he was going to embarrass me or something but he's the one that held the vibrator to my clit, and then he finger fucked me and then," Emma shivered at the memory.

"Oh my god, what'd he do?!" Trinity asked, eagerly.

"After he bit me, he asked if he could taste me. I was out of my mind from the damn pleasure and I just nodded. I thought he was gonna just go back for more blood, but instead, he went downtown and he *feasted*. Trinity, you don't even understand how that vamp *feasted* on me. I can't wait to go back, because I'm going to that same vamp and I'm gonna make him feast again." Trinity's mouth fell open.

"I've never even seen one before. I thought they looked like those hills have eyes creatures," Trinity gasped.

"Oh no. My vamp, he's sexy. Tall. Chocolate. Dark eyes."

"Well damn, why don't you just fuck him them?" Trinity laughed.

"That's the thing. He pays me to drink my blood. But if I wanna ride his dick, I've gotta pay him. That's the way the club works. Eating my pussy is free, depending on the vampire you've got. Like I said, they're sexual beasts. Most of them will feast on you and then thank you and walk away as if you'd given them the blowjob. But because we're human, they want a contract with us to have sex, and contract requires money. That way, if anything goes wrong, they have proof that you agreed to the sex. You couldn't even imagine the false rape allegations those innocent vamps get. It's not fair," Emma sighed. Trinity actually believed that. Some women were just that fucked up.

"When you go again, will you tell me?" Trinity asked. Emma smiled at her.

"Wait, does that mean you want to come with me?" Emma asked.

"Sure. I don't know if I'll let them drink my blood just yet but I want to experience the atmosphere with you. Besides, you know I'm never one for the rules of society. My mother would lose her mind if she knew I went to that club. I think that's a perfect reason to do it," Trinity shrugged.

"That's my girl." Emma leaned over and gave Trinity a high five.

"Now, what are you going to do about this marriage?" Emma asked.

"Girl, I haven't figured it out yet. Let's not even talk about it. I just might lose my own damn mind. Tell me about your vampire. What's his name?"

"Blaze," Emma smiled. "Long dick Blaze. I've seen it. Like a nerd I asked him to show me. And he did. And I nearly passed out. I think he could probably fuck me better than Germaine. And that's saying a lot," Emma said.

"You've got me sold. Now, I want to meet a vampire," Trinity laughed.

Chapter Four

"YOU HAVEN'T FED ALL WEEK, DON'T YOU THINK YOU should get some blood?" Night lifted his eyes from the paperwork on his desk. Blaze entered the large office, licking his lips, the sign that he had just feed. Probably on something more than blood.

"You've been smelling like the same human almost every weekend," Night commented. Blaze flopped down on the large couch and sighed deeply.

"Her blood tastes really good. But her pussy? Man, her pussy is sweet as fuck. I couldn't help myself," Blaze replied with a smile on his face. Night cracked a smile of his own.

"Do you at least know her name?" Night asked.

"Emma. Sweet little Emma. For a human she's very open," Blaze said.

"What you mean?" Night asked.

"Most of these humans come here because they want our money. They take our bite but the moment they leave this place, they turn their noses up at us like they weren't just begging for us to bite them for money. Emma, she takes the bite and the money because she needs it, but she leaves this place and doesn't turn her nose up. She doesn't act like she's better than us and she scolds people when they try to talk down to us. It's cute," Blaze said.

"Two centuries of life and for the first time you have a crush. So cute," Night teased.

"Whatever," Blaze smiled. "Are you gonna feed or not?"

"I have blood saved up in my fridge. I'll be okay," Night shrugged. Blaze shivered.

"That shit is gross and unnatural. The humans thought giving us blood in bags was the only way to keep us quiet. It's fucking nasty. I don't understand why you don't just get a nice human like I found Emma, and drink the natural way and then send her off. It ain't gonna do you harm," Blaze said.

"I haven't drank a woman's blood directly like that since-"

"I know. But it's been 100 years Night. You mustn't do that to yourself. Besides, I'd rather you at least drink from me than drink from those bags." Drinking from a male vampire fulfilled the need of hunger, but for the other needs of a vampire it lacked luster, unless a man was what you preferred.

"I'll only feed from you if I need your strength. Otherwise, it does nothing for me. I'm at full strength and I've been able to live with part of my soul being gone. Blood from a bag does me fine Blaze. Don't worry." Blaze didn't argue with him but he knew that blood from a bag wasn't in the least bit satisfying.

"Can you believe it? Humans thinking blood from a bag is the way to keep us in check?" Blaze scoffed. Truly, over the years times had changed drastically. Especially in the way humans thought. After his beloved died from his bite, Night and Blaze traveled out of Africa altogether. The rest of Night's clan had followed him, wanting to experience another part of the world. They'd settled in New Orleans because they loved the culture of the food. Despite the lore, vampires enjoyed real food as much as they enjoyed blood. Night realized the humans in America were very different from the ones across the ocean in his homeland. Vampires were hoarded into one part of town and treated like scapegoats and animals. Night didn't like it not one bit, and he could have left the moment he realized how his kind was treated, but then he realized the vampires here didn't have anyone fighting for them. Night was already a clan leader and he just cemented his legacy in New Orleans and continued to grow and protect his people as best as he could. This club was one of the ways he was providing a place for vampires to just be vampires. In this part of town, in this club, human rules didn't exist. Humans were at the mercy of their world now, much like the vampires were always at the mercy of humans.

"Let them think what they want. We can only live our life how we need to live it. That's why I've built this place," Night shrugged.

"I fear the vampires here would have died out if we hadn't come here. They didn't have a clan or leader. You did that for them. They feel protected," Blaze said.

"And I wouldn't be able to do it without my oldest friend. Seriously, you're like a thousand years old," Night joked. Blaze took a pillow from the couch and threw it at Night.

"Asshole," Blaze laughed.

"So, are you gonna fuck this human?" Night asked.

"I'm thinking about it. With her tasting as good as she does, I might not even ask her to pay me," Blaze chuckled. The club made money from all the kinky humans who were trying to hide the fact that they wanted no holds barred sex. A separate part of the club catered to those humans who wanted to be tied up, strapped up, and fucked hard. Of course, that part of the club was a secret. Because that's how humans were. Puritans in public but predators and freaks at night. Yet still, the vampires were the so-called dangerous ones. Either way, the club made it so that vampires could feed in their own safe haven and explore sexual relationships that wouldn't backfire on them.

"Just make sure she signs a contract," Night warned.

"I know the rules boss, don't gotta tell me," Blaze said. He stood from the couch.

"Let's strike a deal, vamp," Blaze said, coming towards Night's desk. He placed his hands on the smooth surface and leaned over.

"Really? Striking a deal with me?" Night asked. To strike a deal with a vampire was like a contract that you couldn't break. A promise that you had to fulfill no matter what.

"It's probably the only way to get you out of your own head," Blaze said.

"What you want?" Night asked.

"If I find a woman for you, you've gotta feed from her," Blaze said. Night sat back.

"What if I don't like her?" Night asked.

"Then I'll pick again. But we've been friends a long time Night. I know you're type. So, if I bring a woman in here and you find her attractive, don't fight the attraction and feed from her. that's the deal I'm making with you. I find the girl, you feed from her." Blaze held out his hand. Night shook it firmly.

"Alright fine. You've got a deal."

"Maybe once you get blood from a real vein, you'll let go of that bag blood shit. Besides, I know there's a woman out there for you." Night swallowed. He'd never told Blaze about the dream he had of that mysterious woman named Trinity. When he thought about the woman he'd seen in his dream, he felt his heart pumping and a strange feeling in his body as if his senses were trying to tell him something. Night just didn't know what. After 100 years, one would think he would forget that face, but he never could. Especially when flashes of her would enter his mind at random times.

Rapid knocks on his office door broke the silence between Night and Blaze. Blaze stood and moved behind Night's desk, standing next to Night.

"Enter," Night granted. Another vampire entered, part of Night's clan.

"Another rogue," he reported.

"Did you catch him?" Night asked, worriedly.

"He ran out of vamp town, towards the humans. None of us wanted to step out of that boundary. You know a human so much as sees us on their side of town they have a right to kill us on sight. With the guns and weapons they have against us now, they have a means to actually kill us," he explained.

"Shit," Night cursed. If the humans caught sight of that rogue vampire, they would want to hunt all vampires even though not all of them were rogue."

"Alright, I'll go to human town. Don't worry about it. Blaze will take care of everything here. If you need anything, he's you're go to vamp."

"Shouldn't I go with you?" Blaze asked.

"No. You stay here. I can find the rogue and dispatch of him. A rogue is already enough. If they see two more vampires; they'll start to worry we're trying to take over and it will not go well for us. Besides, I need someone protecting our kind here." Night stood from around his large desk. Behind him in a glass case was his large sword that he'd had for decades. No matter how much time passed, Night wouldn't trade his sword for any automatic weapon.

"You will be able to feel if something has gone wrong Blaze. If you feel so, come find me," Night said. Because they shared a blood bond, they would be able to feel each other's pain, and if either of them died.

Night had already been wearing jeans, so all he had to do was trade in his button up for a t-shirt. He strapped his sword to his back and grabbed the keys to his motorcycle. Night had built this club for the safety of vampires but he didn't stay behind his desk pushing paperwork. He hit the streets and did what he had to do to protect the vampire population. Rogue vampires were dangerous creatures who just lost their souls. It was a terrible sight for Night to see but in the end a rogue vampire couldn't regain his humanity. Not when he'd already crossed that threshold. Night wasn't just protecting vampires from humans. He was protecting them from losing their souls. Somewhere out there was a vampire that Night had failed to protect from themselves.

Chapter Five

"Just stay the night," Emma insisted as Trinity prepared to leave.

"And have my mother blowing up my phone all night? I might as well just go on home. She won't ever leave me alone," Trinity sighed. Emma believed her, she'd seen Rose blow up Trinity's phone, back to back to back. The woman was nonstop.

"You're right. Get on out of here before she calls the police on me again," Emma laughed.

"I can't believe she did that," Trinity shook her head, remembering when her mother had told the police Emma had kidnapped her. It was insane.

"You just be careful. As a matter of fact, call a cab. You can't be walking this time of night. Plus, we were drinking," Emma scolded. As soon as Emma began telling Trinity all about her vampire ventures, Trinity had bust open the liquor and they chatted for hours. Being as coddled as she was while growing up, Trinity never ever dreamed about going to vamp town, and now that Emma was describing this place to her, Trinity was very curious. Vamp town was only a few miles away from Emma's house, across the bayou. Up where Trinity lived vamp town was much further.

"I'm not drunk at all. Besides, you know I like the walk. Gives me time to think. I may run a little bit and call that my exercise. I'll text you while I walk. Don't worry." Trinity gave Emma's cheeks two kisses before she was leaving the house. Trinity only walked for two blocks when she realized that vamp town wasn't that far away. She looked at the watch on her wrist. It was 1am. Smiling deviously, Trinity turned the corner and headed towards vamp town.

Butterflies set loose in her stomach as she walked by the houses leading towards that boundary. When she reached the edge, she paused, looking out into the barren streets. There were unoccupied buildings of businesses that shut down when humans ran from where the vampires would be putting up shop. Windows were boarded up, the streets were abandoned, but Trinity knew if she walked further into town, she'd find the real homes and businesses of the vampires.

"Trinity Kayne? Is that you?" Trinity closed her eyes and cursed. Of course someone recognized her. She couldn't do shit without someone shouting her name. Putting her head down, Trinity turned and walked away from vamp town quickly. She didn't answer the person who had called her name, not wanting to confirm her identity. She hurried off, keeping her head low so no one else was prompted to ask what she was doing so close to vamp town.

When she was far enough where people were minding their own business, Trinity picked up her head and continued to walk, sighing heavily as the humidity produced sweat at her temples. Her roots were already starting to curl up. Nighttime in New Orleans was filled with the sounds of various bugs and insects. Trinity was used to the sounds. But when she heard hissing, now that was different. She slowed down slightly and looked around thinking that maybe there was a lizard nearby. But then again, that had to be a pretty big lizard to hiss that loudly.

"Nope. Not tonight," Trinity stated, picking up her pace. She began to walk faster, refusing to be any lizards midnight snack.

The hissing was sharp and loud, accompanied by a pungent smell. It was like something was rotting. Trinity covered her mouth and broke out into a run. She didn't dare look behind her. Then again, she didn't hear anything but that hissing. She felt a presence at her back, sending off waves of heat at her back. She knew she was in trouble when she felt hot breath skate across her neck. She pumped her legs faster, attempting to outrun whatever was hissing behind her. Sharp claws grazed her shirt, trying to drag her back.

"Argh, urgh!" Trinity grunted as she pushed her legs beyond their limit to run faster. Trinity thought about turning around to swing at whatever was behind her but the thought came too late. Whatever was behind her, pushed her hard. Trinity grunted as she fell forward onto her stomach, the pavement searing her skin. The thing behind her pounced onto her back, hissing into her ear as he breathed heavily on her neck. It's breath was hot and sticky, smelling rotten.

"Blood," he growled. Claws dug into her arms, trying to hold her down as Trinity fought him.

"Get off me you nasty ass fucker!" Trinity snapped, trying to elbow the thing on top of her back, weighing her down. Trinity was fighting with all she could but the thing on top of her weighed a ton and he was rampant on holding her down. Something nicked at her neck, making Trinity still, fear biting through her. Just when she thought her neck would be sliced open, the weight lifted from on top of her. Trinity huffed out as relief emptied from her lungs. She quickly turned around, sitting on the ground and looking for the creature that had attacked her. She gasped and scrambled back as a sword wielding god of a man stalked her attacker. He whispered something softly before he swung the sword, slicing it clean across her assailant's neck. The creature flopped to the ground before smoke began to rise from his severed head. Trinity couldn't help but scream out as the creature burst into flames. Her savior wiped the blood off his sword on his jeans and sheathed it back into the holster across his back. Slowly, he turned around to face her. Trinity scooted back some more, not sure if she should be afraid of the sword wielding man. The shadows of the night hid much of his face, but his build and posture was not easily hidden. He was tall, his waist slim, his body trim, but the muscles of his arms and chest were defined beneath his t-shirt. Even his jeans fit him perfectly.

"You shouldn't walk alone at night. It's dangerous, darling," he spoke, his voice deep and laced with sensuality. Trinity felt a shiver run down her spin.

"Who are you?" Trinity asked. He didn't answer her. She saw his lips form into a sly smile, revealing his sharp fangs. She gasped when she realized that he was a vampire. Trinity finally have proof that vampires didn't look like deformed sickening creatures like she thought. Despite Emma's story, Trinity needed to see for herself and now she was seeing perfectly. The tall vampire in front of her oozed danger, but there was something more. Trinity was entranced. When he backed away, disappearing into the night, Trinity blinked and shook her head trying to snap herself out of her daydreams.

"Oh no you don't," Trinity said popping up off the ground. She chased after him, following where he ducked behind an abandoned house. The house held no occupants, but the light above the backdoor hadn't yet clonked out. Trinity saw him clearer and rushed to catch up with him. She was breathing heavily as she stomped after him, not hiding the fact that she was following him. Just as she reached his back, he turned around sharply. Trinity bumped into his chest and had to force herself not to fall on her ass by the impact.

"Oomph!" She tripped up a little but maintained her

balance. He was definitely strong. And definitely...sexy. She gasped slightly when she stared into his burnt amber eyes.

"Wow," she whispered. Never had she seen eyes of that color before. They were deep and easy to get lost in, but furthermore, they showed so much depth, as if they'd seen a thousand lifetimes already.

"Trinity?" he whispered, his voice more of a question as he stared at her. Night blinked rapidly as the woman who'd haunted his mind now stood in front of him, flesh and blood.

"How—how do you know my name?" she asked. He didn't answer. He closed the small distance between them, keeping them chest to chest. Trinity's breath hitched, feeling her pulse race. Damn. He was more than just good looking. His dark, thick locks, hung in a ponytail down his back, his hairline trimmed so neatly, not one single strand of hair out of place.

"You smile, but the joy doesn't touch your eyes. Why?" he asked.

"Because...I'm not happy with who I have to be," Trinity whispered. She saw when his eyes flickered down to her lips.

"You want to kiss me?" Trinity wasn't sure where that came from. In between the stories of vampires Emma had told her, to the rushing heat below her waist, Trinity couldn't help herself.

"You're bold enough to kiss a vampire?" he asked her, heatedly.

"I'm bold enough to do a lot of things," Trinity shrugged.

"You saved my life. Let me repay you," she said.

"With a kiss?" he asked.

"Show me what you got vamp," Trinity teased. He flashed her a wicked smile. She gasped when he wrapped his arm around her waist and palmed her ass and then put a hand at the back of her neck. He pressed her close, leading her into the kiss. His lips were tender and full, his breath fresh of mint and something sweet. Trinity's body shook as he kissed her deeply, sending waves of burning heat all over her body. When he slid his tongue into her mouth, Trinity just melted. She felt his strained length against her stomach. It was thick and long, trapped behind his jeans. As he slowly pulled away from her mouth, a fang nipped at her bottom lip. It drew the tiniest of blood that he quickly licked up. When he let her go, Trinity stumbled on her own feet.

"You okay, darling?" he asked, his voice having that south lilt but also mixed with something else.

"I've never kissed a vampire," Trinity breathed.

"Come to Club Bitten. I'll do more than kiss you," he stated as he backed away. Trinity tried to control her breathing as the sexy ass vampire who saved her life made her body hot. She blinked, and in that millisecond her eyes were closed, her sexy vampire was gone. Trinity looked all around her, turning in circles. She realized if she wanted to see him again, she'd have to do what he said. Go to club Bitten.

NIGHT USED his powers of being a vampire to move so quickly, that to the human eye it looked like he had simply disappeared. He moved swiftly through the night to where he had left his motorcycle. His heart was hammering heavily, as he revved up the bike and took off. He'd followed that rotten scent of the rogue vampire and closed in quickly on the lost soul. What Night didn't expect was the scent of ripe fruit that began to mingle with the rotten scent of the vampire. Night's natural instinct when he saw the vampire attacking the woman was to jump into action and make sure the woman didn't get bitten. That would be another issue that could see the hunting of vampires again because of human fear.

Once he said a small prayer for the lost vampire, he beheaded the vamp to send him to the afterlife. Night fully intended to just walk away then, but the sound of the human female voice behind him made the hair on the back of his neck stand straight up. Her scent called out to him like a bird singing a song and he just couldn't help himself. Under the light in the back of that house when he saw her face, he literally felt his heart stop for a minute. It was her. Trinity. Was this what his senses had been telling him? That one day he was going to save the beauty from a vicious attack? He thought that was all, but he could sense the arousal and the tightness of her body. He could sense that she wasn't just a normal human who ran away from the unknown. She was daring. She was curious. And she was luscious. The need to kiss her washed over him and that sexual drive inside of all vampires began to burn within him. Even then, he should have just walked away instead of accepting a kiss, because now as he rode home, his lips were tingling with memory of her sweet lips. He would have sucked her blood right then and there if things had been different in their world.

"It's taken care of," Night mumbled as he entered his office inside his club. Blaze shot up from the sofa along with the other vampire who had reported the rogue.

"Thank goodness," he sighed. Night walked by Blaze to put his sword away. Blaze inhaled deeply, his eyes becoming bright yellow before settling down into its natural dark depths.

"Do you know how he turned rogue?" Night asked.

"He overfed. When I took the human away from him, he just went crazy. I thought he was angry and just walked off to cool down. Until I saw the state he was in." There were many ways to go rogue, and feeding on too much blood was the classic. Sometimes vampires didn't know when to stop.

"What happened to the human? And how come I'm just hearing about this now?"

"She ran off. I don't think she's gonna say anything. No human ever wants to admit they come here. You know that, Night."

"We're going to have to double security to make sure no one continues to overfeed. Announce the job opening amongst all the male vampires. Tell them to come to me if they're interested," Night ordered. He quickly nodded and left on Night's orders. Blaze looked at Night.

"You smell like a woman," Blaze said, not even waiting a second before he broached the topic.

"The rogue was attacking a human woman. I intervened in time. I guess her scent got on me," Night replied. Blaze leaned forward and inhaled again.

"No. I smell her on your breath. You kissed her. Didn't you?" Night rolled his eyes and slumped down in his chair.

"I don't know why. Something just came over me. I just followed my instinct, like any vampire would do." Blazed inhaled again.

"Could you stop that! We're vampires not fucking werewolves! Stop smelling me!" Blaze chuckled at Night's reaction but truly, Blaze just wanted to lock that woman's scent into his brain. If he ever caught a small whiff of her scent, Blaze would recognize it immediately and he would make sure to deliver her straight to Night.

Chapter Six

"You wouldn't believe what happened to me last night," Trinity whispered when Emma picked up the phone after only 2 rings.

"What happened? I thought you said you got home fine?" Emma asked.

"I did. But that was after I got attacked by a vampire."

"You what?! And you didn't tell me last night?! All I got was a 'hey, I'm home safe. I'll call you tomorrow, love you Em.' I think you left out a very crucial detail of your night!"

"I know, I know. But I was trying to process it all and then I just fell asleep. Emma, it was fucking crazy. The vampire didn't look right. He was talking about blood and he was damn near on a rampage."

"How in the hell did you get away?" Emma asked.

"Another bad ass vampire with a sword swooped in and saved me. I should have hightailed it when he chopped the other vampire's head off but I didn't. Curiosity got the better of me and I followed him to try and talk to him."

"Oh, you're such a bad girl. What happened next?"

"Emma, he knew my name. I don't know how, but he knew it. And just looking at him, my body got all hot, it's like I was a hormonal teenager again. And then, I dared the man to kiss me!" Emma gasped loudly.

"You've always been brave my friend, but that right there is something else!"

"I don't know, it's like we were playing a cat and mouse thing, and even though he was a complete stranger I felt deep down like me and him were just meant to be in that situation. So, I let him kiss me. And Emma, that man kissed me so good. It's like he knew how I liked to be kissed. I'm telling you this, if he was a demon sent up from hell to trap me, I'll be the devils bitch right now because I fell right into that trap and kissed him like I ain't have no sense." Emma burst out laughing.

"I told you they're sexual creatures Trin!"

"He told me to come to Bitten and he'd do much more to me," Trinity said.

"Oh hell, you gotta go Trinity. At least just one time. I know you're gonna go with me, but if you see your sexy vampire again, you've gotta let him indulge. Like seriously, he could probably suck your pussy until you're in a coma," Emma said.

"I hope you're dressed in there!" Rose banged on Trinity's bedroom door. Trinity scoffed and sucked her teeth.

"I gotta go Emma. I'm having tea time with my future in laws and my damn fiancé," Trinity groaned.

"You are in a world of confusion honey," Emma sighed.

"Talk to you later." She made a kissing sound and hung up the phone. Her mother was still banging on the door, so Trinity stood from her vanity and opened it. Rose looked her up and down.

"See, I'm ready," Trinity replied. Rose gasped and clutched her chest as if she was having a heart attack.

"Oh no. Trinity I know you don't plan to see your future husband in—in this!" Rose exclaimed. Trinity looked down at her jean skirt that held large brass buttons down the front and stopped just a few inches above her knees with a tank top that she tucked into the waist of the skirt to define her slim waist.

"What? I'm going to put a cardigan over the tank top," Trinity said, knowing her breasts were too plump for the tank top alone.

"No. Absolutely not. Undress. Right now." Rose pushed herself past Trinity and went to her closet. Trinity rolled her eyes but she undressed. She just wanted this afternoon over and done with, so she was just going to do whatever they asked of her.

Rose rifled through Trinity's closet and pulled out a sweet looking sundress with colorful flowers. The neckline plunged slightly, only enough to tease but not enough to show too much cleavage. Trinity rolled her eyes again and pulled on the sundress that flared out at her knees. Rose pulled out yellow wedge heels, tossing them to Trinity.

"Now, you look like a humble fiancée. Your hair, let's get it straightened," Rose said.

"No. I draw the line there. I washed it early this morning and perfected my wash n go. I am not straightening these curls. Not today." Trinity's curls dropped along her neck, shrinkage making her hair look shorter than it was, but Trinity loved her hair looking kinky, wild, and short. Anything was better than a flat iron. Rose sensed that she wouldn't win that fight so she dropped it. Picking up a bottle of perfume on the vanity, she sprayed Trinity's neck.

"Good. Now go on and have a good time. Me and your father can't be there to watch your every move, so please; don't mess this up," Rose warned. Trinity grabbed her purse. She wanted to give her mother a mouthful but instead she just smiled one of her fake smiles that she knew looked good to her parents but didn't reveal how unhappy she was. As soon as the feeling crossed her again, she remembered the strange question her vampire had asked her. She smiled, but the joy didn't touch her eyes. A stranger, someone she'd just met saw right through her, but the people who raised her didn't. Or maybe they did and they just didn't care. No one cared. Only Emma cared. But now, this strange vampire cared enough to ask her.

"Trinity do you hear me?" Rose snapped her fingers.

"Yes." Trinity didn't hear but she didn't want a repeat. She left her mother standing in her bedroom so she could get this stupid tea time over and done with.

"OH, YOU LOOK STUNNING MY DEAR," Trent exclaimed when he opened the door. He took her hand and kissed the back of it before guiding her into the house where he kissed her on the lips. Trinity forced herself not to recoil. At least Trent was handsome and she didn't have to be kissed by a frog. He led her into the parlor where his parents were having brunch and sipping on tea.

"Our sweet daughter in law has arrived!" his mother exclaimed, standing to greet her. His father did the same, kissing her on the cheek.

"Careful, dad. She's all mine," Trent smiled. His father chuckled and as he sat down next to his wife. Trent pulled out a seat for Trinity then sat next to her.

"Let's make this official baby," Trent said. He pulled a ring box from his slacks and opened it. The diamond ring was large and sparkling. Any female would fall over seeing dollar signs, but Trinity didn't even care. She sighed and forced a smile to her face as he slipped the ring on her slim finger. She was definitely not going to be wearing this on her own time.

"Let's talk about the wedding and your dress. It's going to be gorgeous I can already see it in my head," his mother swooned. Trinity took a deep breath, getting herself ready to engage in conversation she cared little about.

For three hours, she sipped unsweetened warm tea, ate sugar free cookies, and smiled without much intent as Trent and his parents talked about their future. Trent was already talking about children and Trinity could only bite her tongue and just listen. Trinity thought after tea time she could just run off, but Trent took her hand.

"Let me show you our home," he said.

"Our home?" Trinity asked.

"Yes. Didn't your parents tell you that you'd be moving in with my by the end of the week?" Trent asked. Trinity just blinked at him.

"I take it they did not," Trent sighed.

"Listen-" Trent immediately cut her off.

"Trinity please. I'll listen to whatever you have to say, I promise. But just don't blow up on me in front of my parents. You know they're traditional. Let's go to the house and you can have at me, I promise." His tone of voice was genuine so Trinity went with it.

"Fine," she gritted. Her parents' servants had driven her to the home of Trent's parents but their car was gone when Trinity emerged. Trent took her to his luxury car and opened the door for her. Trinity settled into the seat, crossing her arms, fuming that her parents hadn't even told her that by the end of the week she was expected to live with this man.

Trent was quiet for the entire 15-minute drive to his home. It was just as large as all the other houses in the neighborhood, protected by tall gates. Trent drove up, waved a keycard and the gates swung open. He drove around the circular driveway, parking at the tall front double doors. Trinity kept her mouth shut as Trent guided her inside the house, the foyer was tiled with white tiles and opened up to a beautiful sitting room. Trinity saw his wet bar and immediately walked by him to get herself a drink. His eyes were wide as he watched her pour herself some scotch and throw it back. When she went for the second shot, he stopped her.

"Whoa baby. Easy. Think you can handle all of that?" he asked. Trinity sucked her teeth.

"Who do you think I am Trent? Some prissy little southern girl?" Trinity asked.

"I mean, I know you're not prissy," Trent replied.

"Good. I can handle my liquor. Don't worry about me."

"So, what you want to say to me dear?" Trent asked.

"I'm not the chick you think I am."

"Well then, are you still as headstrong as you were in high school?" Trent asked with a smile. Trinity poured another drink and held out the glass to Trent. He took it and sipped slowly.

"I'm worse," Trinity grinned at him.

"This dress was my mother's way of making me look presentable. But this ain't the way I dress Trent. I like miniskirts and t-shirts. I drink when I feel like it. I like junk food and sweet tea. I cuss. And I speak my mind. I'm also my own woman. I don't like that you asked my parents to marry me instead of asking me. And I definitely don't like that I'm being moved in with you and yet still I had no idea,"

"I'm sorry you feel that way Trinity, but you know how things go here. That's just the way," Trent shrugged.

"As for how you dress, you're fine to dress as you please except when we make public appearances. I'm sure you know that well. Talk to me how you must in private but you will not talk out of line in front of company and you certainly won't curse either. Is that understood?" Trent asked. Trinity just looked at him. She didn't expect any different. He was a man that was raised in this community. They all thought they were the shit and ruled the damn world.

Trinity poured herself another drink and sat in one of the

matching chairs next to the bar. She took a few sips before sighing and looking at him.

"You expect us to really be married, don't you?" Trinity asked him.

"Yes, I do. I hope you feel the same Trinity because this can be very complicated. Especially since I have already booked our venue and paid for it. I'm sure you parents would not want to go through the stress of being tied up in legal discourse if this wedding goes wrong," Trent replied.

"Legal discourse?" Trinity asked.

"We have a contract. An agreement. If the wedding doesn't go as planned, my family will sue yours for all you've got. I'm sure you don't want that to happen." Trinity was even more stunned to hear this was mostly legal and not tradition. Now things were more serious. Her parents could lose their livelihood over this. Then again, it wouldn't be her fault. They shouldn't have signed any legal contract without talking to her. Trinity was beyond frustrated.

"So, you move in at the end of the week and that's that really. We don't need any troubles. Do we?" Trent asked. Trinity didn't like his tone of voice. Almost like he knew he had won.

"Alright. I move in. You get what you want. Now. Am I allowed to get what I want?" Trinity asked.

"What do you want dear? I will gladly give it to you," Trent replied. Trinity leaned back.

"Pull your dick out and let me see," Trinity said. Trent chuckled.

"Excuse me?"

"You want me to move in. Plus, I have to get married to you. I need to know what it is I'm getting married to. I need to be prepared. So, pull it out. Let's go. Don't tell me you're afraid of your fiancée seeing your dick. However will we function as husband

and wife?" Trinity asked. Trent stared at the beauty that sat in the chair across from him. She was nothing like the women he liked to have because she did her own thing and she didn't listen. Trent liked the females who did what he said and worshipped his presence. Trinity was carefree and easy spirited. She said what was on her mind. That's probably why Trent wanted her. She would be hard to control but she was drop dead gorgeous and he had an inkling that her attitude in public turned into wild seduction at night. Trent was beyond smitten. He just had to have her. The only way he knew to do that was involving legal terms. Now there was nothing that could disrupt what they would have.

"You're an enigma, Trinity," Trent smiled. He undid his slacks, slowly unzipping them. Trinity sat back with a smile on her face while she sipped her drink. Trent pulled down his underwear and let his dick pop out, unafraid of showing her what he had to offer. Trinity's brows popped up, clearly impressed.

"You're not a sad case after all," Trinity said. She threw back her drink and gulped it down. Standing, she shimmied out of her sundress. Trent watched with heated eyes as her plump breasts shook in her bra. She was wearing a matching purple thong to her purple bra. Her ass moved so fluidly, Trent had to wipe sweat from his brow.

"Okay, come on. Where's the bedroom? Or you wanna get kinky right here?" she asked, sitting down with her legs wide open.

"I know you're not suggesting we have sex before we're married!" Trent gasped. Trinity made a face.

"I don't care what legal shit you got going on with my parents Trent. But I'm not marrying you, unless you're a good fuck. We can call this the practice run," Trinity smiled devilishly.

"Don't look so shocked Trent. Oh, and I'm not a virgin by the way. So, you can let that dream go," Trinity waved him off.

Trent stared at her, grinding his teeth. He wanted to be her first and only but truthfully, he knew that would be farfetched.

"Alright fine. Let's go fuck. You'll be dying to marry me once we're done," he stated. Trinity rolled her eyes at him but he was already walking away. She stood from the chair and followed him, uncaring that she was nearly naked.

Trent led the way to the master bedroom, using both hands to open the double doors. The bed was high and large, just like Trinity figured he probably slept in. Trinity pushed by him and climbed the three small steps to lead up to the bed. She flounced down on the mattress, looking out at Trent. He was just watching her, his arousal beginning to grow in his pants that were still unzipped. Trinity was actually surprised he had a good-sized dick. Maybe that's why he acted the way he did. Leaning back on her elbows, Trinity crossed her legs at the ankles then slowly lifted them in the air before uncrossing them and opening them wide slowly. Trent's nose flared as his eyes bulged from his head. He slowly began to unbutton his grey shirt and shook it off. He undressed in front of her and Trinity just gazed at him, a small smile etched on her face.

He yanked down his pants, kicked out of his shoes and socks before he walked towards the bed. Instead of using the stairs like she did, he just hopped onto the bed, crawling towards her open legs. Trinity quickly pressed her foot against his chest to stop him.

"No glove, no love," she winked. His mouth nearly turned into a snarl.

"You do all this teasing and now you want me to wear a condom?" he asked.

"We're not married yet honey. Just because I have to sample your dick game, doesn't mean I have to let you bust inside me." Trent scowled at her, but even from where he was he could smell the sweetness of her skin and though he didn't want to admit it, he wanted her bad.

"Fine," he grunted. He hopped back off the bed and walked across the room, disappearing into the bathroom. He returned with the condom already strapped tight to his length. His face was bone straight, like a man on a mission. This time, Trinity didn't stop him when he hopped onto the bed. He yanked at her ankle, dragging her towards him.

"Whoa, you're rough," Trinity chuckled at him. He opened her legs and yanked down her thong nearly ripping it. Trinity could already see that he was going to be rough all around because he thought he had to prove his own masculinity. He pulled down her bra and leaned forward, sucking her nipple into his mouth. He bit down, yanking the nipple with his teeth.

"Ouch! They're not gumballs!" Trinity exclaimed, not liking the sensation whatsoever.

"You asked for it," he grunted. He climbed on top of her, shoving her legs open. His kisses were rough against her skin and Trinity didn't know what the hell he thought he was doing but it had no effect at all. He clasped a hand around her throat and forced her to look at him. He licked along her neck before he rose up and kissed her lips rough. Trinity tried to deepen the kiss, trying to capture the same essence of the kiss she had shared with the vampire but she was let down instantly. Trent's lips didn't move in the same way. His tongue flicked in and out of her mouth in a strange way that reminded her of a damn lizard and he was panting heavily inside of her mouth like he couldn't catch his damn breath. He didn't allow her to control the kiss so she was forced to accept his strange mouth movements. Her eyes were open and she was just staring at him, waiting for the kiss to be over. Finally, when he pulled away from her, he gulped as if he'd been swimming under water. He hooked her legs over his shoulder, aiming his tip at her entrance. She was wet because of her own natural juices, but none of them had come from him. Trent didn't seem to care. He pressed the protected head of his dick in her entrance, slowly entering her.

Trinity actually gasped, his size well accommodating to drive a reaction out of her. But instead of pushing in as much as he could have, he stopped halfway and pulled out, giving her short, quick strokes. Trinity felt her neck crick as she tilted her head and looked at him.

"Damn Trinity, I always knew you'd feel so damn good," he groaned.

"I can't imagine how you're feeling me," Trinity said, cutting her eyes at him. He groaned and grunted as he grinded inside of her. Trinity felt laces of pleasure, but it all fell short. She needed the whole thing. She tried to scoot down and meet him thrust for thrust.

"Oh no baby, I'm in control here," he stated, holding her down. Trinity laid there, her mouth agape. There just had to be a catch. Brotha had a nice looking dick, but here he was, fucking her like he was 13 and didn't know he could put the whole thing inside her. Trinity squeezed her muscles tight trying to gain some pleasure, trying to force her body to feel more than he was giving her.

"Fuck, I'm about to come," he growled.

"WHAT?!" Trinity screeched.

"Oh no, oh hell no!" She pushed at him hard until her legs fell from his shoulders. He was startled by the movement and Trinity used that to her advantage. She slithered out from under him.

"Lay down," she ordered.

"I told you that I'm-"

"And I said lay down!" Trinity snapped at him, nearly taking his head off. Trent glared at her but then he finally laid back, his dick jutting out towards the ceiling. Trinity swung her leg over his hip and aligned herself with his erection. His hands went to her hips as she started to slide down.

"Not so much!" he shouted. Trinity ignored him and slide down completely, finally making his erection touch that soft spot inside of her. Trent's hips jerked.

"Ugh, argh, urgh!" he shouted, holding her hips as his hips jerked from under her. Trinity looked down at him, her brows furrowed.

"What in the fuck was that?" Trinity asked. His body went laxed as he smiled.

"If you didn't force me to wear this damn rubber, you'd know exactly what to was," Trent sighed. Trinity's mouth fell open again and then she began to feel him soften. She rose up and he flopped out of her, the condom full of his release.

"You have got to be kidding me," Trinity gasped.

"I told you not so much but you didn't want to listen," he said. Trinity rolled her eyes and climbed off his dick.

"Now, I'm gonna drop you home and you're gonna get your stuff packed to move in. understood?" he asked, getting out of the bed. Trinity had no words. Her so called fiancé couldn't fuck, and he barely lasted ten minutes. He couldn't even kiss.

"Do you hear me, Trinity?" he asked.

"I heard you," she waved him off. She scooted off the bed and went hastily to the bathroom to clean herself up. This was a damn disaster.

Chapter Seven

"IF WE DIDN'T DO IT THIS WAY, YOU WOULD HAVE NEVER went along with this marriage," Rose tried to explain to her daughter. Trinity had given her parents the silent treatment for the rest of the week. For one, she was very much angry that Trent had left her unsatisfied and frustrated, and then for two, her parents had struck up a legal contract for her to marry Trent. She felt suffocated all the way through no matter where she turned.

"Just talk to us," James tried to urge his first born as he watched her pack a small bag of her things to move in with Trent.

"I'm leaving the rest of my stuff here. I'm only bringing this suitcase and that's it. If I feel like coming back for any reason, you're to allow me to stay. Can you do that?" Trinity asked.

"You can always come back and stay with us dear. Besides, all of these things Trent can buy you new ones," Rose tried to assure her. Trinity flopped down on her bed and picked up her motorcycle magazine. She flipped it open and stopped at the page she'd doggy eared. It was a Harley-Davidson Softail classic. She wanted to buy the bike herself, but even though her parents were rich, she wasn't. Even just taking money from her trust fund, Trinity needed a good reason otherwise the action was blocked.

"It could be a wedding gift if things go as planned," James said, pointing to the picture of the motorcycle he knew his daughter loved. His oldest was the exact opposite of both him and her mother. They enjoyed wine, she liked beer and shots, they loved golf, she loved watching football. They loved tea time and she preferred lemon cakes and sweet tea while sitting in the hot sun. They enjoyed luxury cars and comfort, and she wanted to ride motorcycles as if she lived in some place like Austin. They'd never been able to connect to their daughter. They were just too different.

"First you sign a contract without telling me and now you're trying to bribe me with something you know I really want," Trinity shook her head.

"Trent is a good man. We would never force you into a marriage with a man that wouldn't be beneficial. You just have to trust us," Rose said.

"I'm done trusting either of you," Trinity admitted. It made no sense. Her parents would never take her feelings into consideration. As evil as it all was, Trinity didn't just want to walk out of this whole marriage thing knowing that her parents could lose everything. Even she wasn't that cruel. Yet, her parents didn't seem to realize that.

"We're stuck in the contract. So, this is the way it has to be Trinity. You understand that," James said. Trinity snapped her magazine close and stood. She closed her suitcase and snatched up her backpack. She pushed by her parents with her luggage and left her bedroom. She couldn't stand to hear this anymore. In the driveway, she packed her bags into the family car where their driver was already seated behind the wheel. She hopped into the backseat.

"I'm ready," she said distantly.

"Of course, Miss Kayne," he replied, putting the car in gear and driving off. Trent was waiting at the front doors when the car pulled around the circular driveway to his home. Trinity forced her eyes not to roll as she slipped from the car. She lugged her things from the trunk and towards the front door.

"Welcome home dear," he smiled cockily.

"Where are the rest of your things?" he asked, taking her suitcase from her and closing the front door.

"This is all I need for now. Where's the guest room?" she asked.

"Guest room? You are something else dear," he chuckled. Trinity made a face.

"Look, stop with all that 'dear' shit. We're not some white family from the 50s. Cut it the fuck out. And yes, the guest room. One, because I'm being forced to live here, and two, because the last time I was in the master bedroom you didn't give me the orgasm you thought you could. I saw the legal contract you have with my parents. I'm to stay in this house but it doesn't specify where. So, where's the guest room?" Trinity asked. Trent looked at her long and hard.

"Alright Trinity. We're gonna play this your way. The guest rooms are in the left wing of the house. Pick any that you choose. We have a live-in servant that occupies the guest room near the back of the house next to the kitchen. Don't' be frightened when you see her. She'll be preparing dinner in a few hours. I have work to do in my office, so you will not see me until dinner." Trent leaned forward and kissed her. Trinity tried to back away but he wrapped his hand around the back of her neck and forced her to accept the kiss.

"I'll play this game with you Trinity, but only because I'm gonna love to see the look on your face when you lose," Trent grinned. He kissed her forehead.

"You be a good girl, alright? And wear something nice for dinner." He patted her ass and walked away, after winking at her.

"Jerk," Trinity grumbled. She rolled her suitcase towards the left side of the house. She entered a hall, carpeted with an expensive looking carpet runner. There were three guest bedrooms on this side. Trinity choose the one all the way at the end of the hall. She realized that around the corner from the room, it opened up to the corridor that led to the kitchen and then the back door. She had an inkling that the easy accessible backdoor would provide solace to her when she needed to get away from being suffocated. With Trent, she knew she wouldn't be able to breathe.

Closed off in the bedroom, she sighed and sat on the stool in front of the dresser equipped with a large mirror. She looked at her wild hair, her perfect twist out, shrinking with the humidity, but still Trinity loved it. She pulled her shrunken bang from her face and pinned it away. She looked at herself in the mirror. She had bags under her eyes but she wasn't physically tired. She wasn't wearing makeup, not that she truly ever did. Trent would probably be up her ass trying to force her to wear makeup when he wanted to show her off.

"Mrs. Trinity Michaelson," Trinity said the name aloud with a smile. The name that would be hers in a couple of months if she didn't change something. Married to Trent. She couldn't believe it. Trinity studied her smile. It was bright, it was sweet, it showed off her white teeth and her southern charm. Her eyes however were dull, drowning in sorrow and pleading for help. No, her smile didn't touch her eyes.

You smile, but the joy doesn't touch your eyes, why? The voice of her mysterious vampire crawled across her mind. She didn't know why, but something flirted across her heart when she thought about that dark, deep kiss. All the things Emma had told her about vampires raided Trinity's mind. Jumping from the chair she retrieved her laptop from her bag. She hopped on the bed and opened her computer to search everything she could about vampires. Her interest was definitely piqued.

"AND WHERE ARE YOU GOING?" Trent was leaning in the doorway of her new bedroom, a glass of scotch in his hand. His servant had created a gumbo that Trinity very much appreciated. Her mother made healthy, light dinners like they didn't live in the damn south. Vickie, the 40-year-old servant was thick and talked only of fattening Trinity up so she could carry big healthy babies. Trent had only smiled proudly at his servant while she set the table for dinner. Trinity indulged in the hearty meal with no remorse but she knew once it was over she had her plans for the night. She'd slipped out of her bodycon dress and brushed her teeth to freshen her breath from the gumbo. When she left the adjoining bathroom, there Trent was, leaning on the doorframe.

"I'm going to Emma's house," Trinity replied as she picked out a jean skirt and a crop top t-shirt.

"Oh, I remember Emma. You two are still friends? She's pretty low on the income scale, isn't she?" Trent asked.

"You can't measure the quality of a relationship based on money," Trinity said.

"I should have known you'd say something like that. I mean, I suppose I don't have a problem with it. Your parents told me you often went out at night to hang with friends. I just didn't know it was Emma. You can be friends with her, but she can't be invited to any of our events." Trinity let out a hearty laugh. This man definitely thought he was somebody's daddy.

"You're funny, Trent. Emma's my best friend. Which means she's my maid of honor. So, keep thinking she won't be seen around with us," Trinity rolled her eyes.

"What is it that you and her are going to do? It's almost 8. I can't imagine what two females would be doing at this time of night," Trent said.

"We're going to drink and talk about how fucked up our lives are and I'm going to feast on Emma's sticky lemon cake." Trinity smacked her backside.

"That cake is how I got this ass," Trinity winked. Trent actually chuckled.

"You're one of a kind Trinity. You can go have time with your friend. I have business meetings early in the morning, I'll be in bed when you come back. But please, take one of my cars. I will not have my fiancée taking cabs or worse; walking."

"You're so generous," Trinity said sarcastically. Trent didn't pick up on her tone.

"Want to leave me with a parting gift?" Trent asked her, his eyes raking up and down her body. Trinity snorted and tried to hold back her laughter.

"No," she chuckled. "Not until you learn some moves man,"

"I don't know what you mean," Trent said with his brows jutted down.

"Two words. Deep. Stroke." Trinity grabbed her clutch and stuffed it with essentials. Trent stood there looking dumbfounded as Trinity pecked him on the cheek to show him the little love she knew his ego probably needed. She hummed as she walked towards the kitchen where she'd seen the row of keys hung on the back wall next to the back door. She grabbed the set with the silver horse keychain, always wanting to drive a mustang.

———

"DAMN IT! The lemon cake isn't done yet!" Emma exclaimed when she opened the door, to see Trinity leaning against the wooden rail around her porch.

"Sorry sis, I just had to leave as soon as I could."

"New house not looking so great?" Emma asked. Trinity hadn't turned around yet, looking out at the darkness of the land around Emma's house.

"The house is great actually. Beautiful. But how can I appreciate it when I don't even want to be there? And what? Should I just say to hell with what my parents worked hard for and say fuck the contract that could sue them so hard they're pissing in pans for the rest of their lives?" Trinity asked.

"No matter how hard it gets, you're too much of a caring person to allow that kind of thing to happen to your folks, even if they are fucked up. But at the same time, you can't possibly lock yourself in a marriage that will make you miserable. Aren't you tired of the act?" Emma asked. Trinity didn't answer for a moment.

"I can't get the police involved either. My parents damn near pay their salary, they just eat out of my parents' hands. They wouldn't do anything about this," Trinity added.

"So then what are you going to do?" Emma asked her.

"Find out what I really want," Trinity replied.

"What do you want right now?" Emma questioned. This time, Trinity turned around and looked at her best friend. She smiled deviously.

"Well, I want some sweet tea and lemon cake. And then, I want you to take me to club Bitten, Trinity said, giving Emma a wink.

Chapter Eight

Blaze watched as humans came and went from the club, each having those pleasured grins on their faces. He thought humans were so hypocritical. *What if they eat our children? What if they feed off of us when we're asleep? What if they rape our women and make vampire babies? What if they erase our memories or put us under a mind control spell?* Those were all the things plus more that the humans had cried about, in their fear against vampires. Blaze found it incredibly vain that humans thought vampires lived just to butt into human business; like the humans were the reason vampires existed in the first place. Yet, here the humans were, leaving with smiles slapped to their ugly mugs because a vampire had pleasured them.

Back in the day human blood was pure and sweet. Now, it was filled with toxins, drugs, and fat. Still, vampires drank their blood and used whatever they could of it. Blaze couldn't find his proper fill until he'd sipped from Emma. He never cared about why humans came to the club, but after sipping her fresh blood, all of a sudden, he was curious about her whole life. He was saddened to hear she was doing this for the money, or else her home would be foreclosed on. Blaze had never cared about a human until her. His obsession became worse when he realized that Emma wasn't stuck up, and stupid like most other humans. It's why his ass was paying close attention to the door, anticipating her arrival. It was the best part of his week. She only came in on weekends, and Blaze damn near wanted her to come every day. He could just ask her on a date. Humans liked that shit. Blaze wondered if she'd want to be seen in public with him.

Blaze sat at the bar and watched the door. He took several drinks of whiskey. He was unable to get drunk, but he still admired the taste of the alcohol across his tongue. Slim arms wrapped around him.

"Need a drink?" the woman pressed her salty lips to his ear and whispered. Blaze shrugged her off easily.

"No honey. I think you've had enough for the night," Blaze said. He snapped his fingers, motioning to one of the security guards. The human's eyes were glazed over, a sign that she was fresh from being fed off of. She was high off the pleasure of the bite and was seeking more like some sort of addict. The security guard whisked her away, carrying her out of the club. As the guard left, Blaze caught the scent he craved. He stood abruptly as Emma entered the club. She was wearing a black silk dress that hung loosely from her body, but Blaze knew that curves were hidden behind that fabric. Blaze chugged the last of his drink and left the bar immediately. Emma was looking around the club, trying to spot him out. He readily walked towards her. When she spotted him, her eyes sparked awareness and she smiled brightly.

"My sweet Emma. You've come back to me," Blaze greeted her.

"I hardly think you can keep me away," Emma smiled. Blaze wrapped an arm around her waist and kissed her neck softly. His dick was already getting hard at the thought of tasting her sweet blood.

"Just wait a little moment Blaze. I want you to meet some-one," Emma said.

"Who?" Blaze looked behind Emma but didn't see anyone of importance. Emma turned around and tugged on the arm of a woman who was just a bit taller than Emma and had a head of wild curly hair.

"Stop gawking and come on," Emma ordered. She pulled the woman next to her and motioned towards Blaze.

"This is Blaze," Emma introduced. The woman looked Blaze up and down, her eyes expressive and fiery.

"Whoa, Emma. No wonder you're sprung. He's a walking wet dream," she exclaimed. Blaze gazed at her, surprised by her attitude. Someone walked behind her and pushed her closer to Blaze. He took a deep whiff of her scent. She was the one.

"Not saying that all vampires know each other but I met one and he told me to come here to see him. I'm wondering if you know him. Dark skin. Long thick locks. Sexy as all hell. Kisses like the devil. Seen him?" she asked. Blaze smiled slightly, showing the tips of his fangs.

"Is this a good friend of yours, Emma?" Blaze asked.

"My best friend, in fact," Emma replied.

"Go wait for me in our special room my sweet Emma. I'll take care of your friend." Emma shivered at the kiss Blaze pressed to her neck. He shooed her along with a pat on the butt.

Trinity should have been afraid when the tall vampire locked eyes with her, but she knew that Emma wouldn't leave her alone with a dangerous creature. Besides, the way he kissed Emma reflected tenderness.

"You know the vampire I'm describing?" Trinity asked. He winked at her and held his hand out. Trinity lifted her hand slowly. She was trying to convince herself that this was a bad idea, but it didn't work. She slipped the vampire her hand and he served her a wicked grin before whisking her away.

NIGHT WAS LEANING against his desk, his arms crossed, brows furrowed as he looked at the young vampire in front of him. The vamp was only a teen, and had yet learned to control his sexual urges.

"What is the number one rule for the club?" Night asked.

"No sex without a contract," he grumbled. Night picked up the contract from his desk that was bare of a signature.

"Here's your contract, without a signature, yet the guards found you having sex with a human," Night said.

"I'm sorry Night! I was gonna make her sign it after! But it was all hot and heavy and she started stroking me, and then sucking me, I couldn't stop," he exclaimed. Night knew he couldn't punish the young male too much because he understood that passion was an easy trap for a teen vampire.

"What do you think your punishment should be then? You know your mother is going to freak the fuck out, right?"

"Don't tell her Night! She won't ever let me come back!" He shrieked.

"How old was that girl?" Night asked.

"17, like me," he replied. Night sighed and rubbed his eyes.

"Jasp, you know the human world has different rules. We've went over this countless of times. You cannot have sex with any human female unless she's 18," Night said. Jasp looked around the room uneasily. Night could feel the rising panic in the young vampire.

"Are they gonna say I raped her?" he asked.

"If her parents find out that's exactly what they're gonna say. Hell, if she feels like it she can say you raped her. And we have no proof that you didn't because you didn't make her sign the contract. It'll be her word against yours and in a human court guess who's side they're gonna choose?" Night asked.

"Please Night, I didn't mean for this to happen. I won't ever do it again but don't let them take me off to some human prison," Jasp begged.

"You're part of my clan Jasp. You know I will fight tooth and nail for you. As for your punishment, you're to help out the staff for three hours a day until I tell you to stop. Also, you're never to see that girl again. If she comes back to the club and wants to see you, you need to come get me immediately so I can talk with her. If you're feeling the weight of your hormones come out of control, you can always come to me and I can help you. Do you understand?" Night asked.

"Yes! Yes, thank you Night. Without my dad around, things can get tough for me. All my other friends know how to control themselves, except for me. It's hard." Rapid knocks sounded at the office door. Instead of waiting for an answer, Blaze burst through the door.

"There's only one vampire who would dare to knock and still come in, uninvited," Night chucked. Blaze smiled.

"Hey kid," he said, plucking Jasp at the ear.

"Fangs feeling a little bit better?" Blaze asked him.

"Yeah. My mom put whiskey on it," Jasp replied. At age 17, the vampire started his second wave of maturity, his fangs getting longer and thicker and sometimes that resulted in aching gums almost like a teething baby.

"Remember our deal Night?" Blaze asked.

"Oh hell," Night groaned, knowing his oldest friend probably brought with him some woman that Night was going to ultimately refuse.

"You can come in," Blaze called out, looking towards the door.

"I can already tell you right now that I'm not-" Night froze when Trinity walked into the office. She didn't walk in like she was afraid or nervous, she walked in like she owned the place. Her chin was high, her eyes bright with curiosity.

"Wow, check this place out," she gasped. She brought her

eyes straight to Night and his heart pounded loudly. They shared a moment, just gazing at each other, blinking and breathing.

"If it isn't my vampire in shining armor," Trinity smiled.

"Trinity," he breathed.

"We never got around to you explaining how you know my name? I'm very curious," Trinity said, closing the distance between them. Night was continually shocked that she wasn't the least bit afraid of him or where she was. She closed the distance on three vampires and shrugged it off like she was around her own kind.

"Damn," Jasp whispered. Night looked at the young vampire sharply and snapped his fingers at him.

"Cut that out," Night snapped.

"Sorry," Jasp held his head down and backed away from Trinity who was sparking his hormones.

"I don't mean to snap at you Jasp, I apologize. I know you can't help it," Night sighed, knowing he shouldn't have had that reaction but having another male appreciate Trinity's beauty definitely made him territorial.

"It's okay," Jasp shrugged. Night tore his eyes from Trinity and kept his gaze on Jasp.

"When does my punishment start?" Jasp asked.

"Tomorrow morning. Enjoy the rest of the night. But be careful. I don't want you mixed with anything you shouldn't be mixed with. Think you can handle that?" Night asked.

"I think I'll be okay. Thanks for not locking me up. Ma says as clan leader if I give trouble you can lock me in the dungeon for days and she wouldn't be able to save me," Jasp said. Both Blaze and Night laughed.

"Your mother thinks of the old days. I'd never lock you up Jasp. I'm here to protect you and your mother until you are old enough to protect yourself and your mother all on your own. But if you make that silly mistake again, I'll tear your fangs out," Night warned. Jasp went straight with fright before he began to back up slowly.

"I'll just go stay out of trouble," Jasp said before he was dashing out of the office. Night chuckled and looked back at Trinity.

"Well, I'll leave you two alone. And don't tell me that she's not the one Night because she's the one I smelled all over you," Blaze said, walking out of the office, letting Night know he didn't want to hear any excuses. Then, Trinity and Night were left alone.

"Ripping out his fangs. That's pretty mean," Trinity said. Night shrugged.

"Standard punishment. Besides, they grow back," Night replied. He pointed to the seat in front of his desk.

"Please, sit," he said. Trinity obeyed, moving swiftly as she sat down.

"Would you like anything to eat? Anything to drink Darling?" he asked her.

"Surprise me," Trinity shrugged. Night smiled at her before picking up a tablet on his desk. He scrolled and touched on the screen for a moment before he set it down and looked at her again.

"So, you're a clan leader huh? Means you're the top dog? The boss?" Trinity asked.

"It just means that I have people that count on me to protect them," Night replied.

"Like that vampire? How old was he anyway? Looked like a teenager."

"Yes, just like him. He's only 17. Good kid. But at that age vampires are very hormonal. They're in their second stage of puberty. Our fangs get larger and he's in the mindset that he has to dominate a female to be seen as a male of worth."

"Dominate?" Trinity asked, scrunching up her nose.

"Why does the strength of the man rely on them being able

to dominate a woman? Where's the logic? Of course he can dominate a female if he's physically strong enough. And where's the chivalry in that? I see, a man who tests his strength on dominating women is just a pussy," Trinity shrugged. Night's eyes widened in his head. He hadn't ever heard a woman talk in that way but he knew the new age of woman was very different. He might have been offended if it wasn't Trinity.

"You misunderstand me darling," he finally spoke.

"Oh? So, make me understand vamp," she said, crossing her legs.

"Vampire women like to be dominated. Not in terms of being controlled or told what to do. They liked to be dominated sexually. If a man can't dominate her and pleasure her in that way, she doesn't see any worth in him and thinks he's a child. Jasp is now trying to prove his worth to women in that way because he's almost on the verge of being a grown vampire male."

"Oh," was all Trinity could say. She felt silly for her outburst but knew human men thought that way.

"You dominate woman then?" she asked him. He looked at her, his dark eyes sparking amber for a quick second.

"Only if I'm trying to prove a point. But I'm an old vampire, I don't have to prove my worth in that way."

"So, you're a lazy fuck then?" Trinity smiled. Night leaned forward, hovering in her space. Trinity gasped and sat back, her eyes for a moment only paying attention to his lips.

"Ask me to dominate you Trinity, and I will," he said darkly.

"Think you can handle me?" Trinity stuttered, trying to catch her breath. Night chuckled, his deep voice vibrating through her.

"I've never met any woman like you before," Night said.

"Because I'm one of a kind," Trinity smiled. Night leaned forward, closing that final distance between them. He pulled her lips into a deep kiss that stole her breath away, yet again. Her heart hammered in her chest as arousal leaked between her legs, soaking the skimpy thong she wore. His locks fell around them, enclosing them with a sweet vanilla scent. However old of a vampire he was, he smelled good as fuck. Trinity kissed him back, desperately, earnestly as if this was the man she was supposed to wed and she wanted to prove how much she wanted him. When her clit began to throb, she painfully yanked away from his kiss and touching her mouth with her fingers, looking at the vampire that leaned in front of her.

"I sense desperation on your lips darling," Night told her. Trinity was speechless, just looking at the sexy man in front of her wondering if it would be completely out of this world if she tore his clothes off and fucked him.

"Maybe I am," she breathed. A soft knock at the door interrupted them.

"Enter," Night granted, finally leaning away from Trinity. Trinity finally felt like she could take a deep breath. A waiter entered the office, rolling a large tray with two alcoholic drinks that looked like Hurricane's, what New Orleans was famous for and two plates of food, covered with a dome. The waiter lifted the domes before nodding and leaving the office.

"That's what you did on your tablet?" Trinity asked. Night nodded as he retrieved the plates of food and the drinks and placed them on his desk. Trinity scooted her chair up so she could eat comfortably from his desk.

"Fried shrimp. You really know how to win a southern girl's heart," Trinity smiled.

"When you've lived long enough you learn all the tricks," Night said. Trinity watched as he sat in his chair behind his desk and picked up his shrimp. She watched with hungry eyes as his thick lips wrapped around the piece of fried food.

"You're staring," Night said.

"I just—I just didn't know vampires eat food," Trinity

replied, trying to find any excuse but the real reason she was staring at the man.

"We are very different from what is portrayed of us. Blood sustains us but ultimately if I don't eat food I can starve, lose weight, become malnourished. Blood is what drives our life-force but we enjoy a meal just like anyone else," Night replied.

"I should have known not to be so naïve. Shame on me."

"Don't talk down on yourself Trinity," he stated. Trinity paused midchew to look at him. It was clearly an order but his tone of voice and body language wasn't forceful like Trent's would have been.

"How do you know my name, yet I don't know yours?" Trinity asked.

"Night," he replied.

"That's your name?" she asked. Night nodded.

"How did that come to be?" she questioned.

"My mother said when I was born, I came out dark as night," Night chuckled. Trinity giggled, covering her mouth before food came flying out at this sexy ass man. Night reached for a napkin and leaned forward, reaching out to wipe sauce from her chin. As he did so, his knuckle brushed against her soft lips. Night couldn't help the reaction he had. His eyes burned amber and his fangs began to dip from his gums.

"Can I see them?" Trinity whispered. Night lift his lips, showing off his teeth to her. Trinity wasn't shy about touching his teeth. She knew they were sharp, but actually feeling them made it all real. She pressed her thumb to the sharp points without thinking.

"Ouch!" She squealed when they pricked her too hard, drawing blood.

"Darling you have to be careful," Night warned her. He took her hand and flicked his tongue out, licking the blood from the prick and healing her at the same time. A shiver poured down Trinity's back at the feel of his tongue. It was only one flick, but damnit, her clit throbbed. She swallowed and fanned herself.

"Are you warm?" he asked her.

"Oh yeah," she breathed, taking her hand from his grasp. She took several deep breaths and reached for her Hurricane that had at least 6 different types of rum. It warmed her throat and electrified her body. Drinking this around Night was a bad idea. The moment Trinity realized it was a bad idea, she eyed the glass and took another large gulp.

"When you rescued me, you called me by my name. But how'd you know my name? What? Did you read my mind or something?" Trinity asked him, trying to change the subject.

"Despite the folklore, vampires can't read minds. We can communicate through mind speak but that's not the same as reading minds. I can alter your perception of an event but I can't ultimately erase your memory. At some point or another, you'd regain the memory I erased. For instance, if I fed from you, I can tell you that you only took a stroll in the park and we never met. It wouldn't of course change the fact that you'd know you were fed from. Only really old vampires do that though. The human mind is harder to manipulate in these days. We can very easily decipher a lot about a person through touch. Things that most humans wouldn't know until you expressed it to them or asked them."

"How did you know my name them?"

"I had a dream about you. A premonition if you will. And then I heard your name in my mind," Night shrugged.

"Did you know I was going to be attacked?" Trinity asked.

"No actually. The premonition was just of you smiling but I saw no happiness in your eyes. You were smiling to please others, not because you were pleased," Night replied. Trinity took another sip of her drink.

"That should freak me out. But oddly enough, I'm not freaked out," Trinity shrugged.

"You did say you were one of a kind, didn't you?" Night asked with a smile.

"Aren't you going to drink your drink?" Trinity asked.

"I don't want it," he said blatantly, waving off the drink. Truthfully that tiny drop of blood that he'd swept away from Trinity's thumb with his tongue was stuck on his taste buds. He wanted more. Damn, he'd never wanted to drink from a female this badly.

"Why'd you come here, Trinity?" he asked her.

"Because you told me to come here, and you'd do more to me than just kiss me," she replied. Night slowly stood from his chair. He put his hands in his jeans pockets and walked around the desk until he was leaning against the front of the desk, looking right at her. Trinity decided to stand. He had several inches on her, but standing just made her feel better equipped to handle whatever he would do to her.

"I guess I needed to come here to do something I wanted to do for a change," she shrugged. Night wrapped an arm around her waist and pulled her close to him. Trinity melted against his body as he ran his fingertips along her arms, and then her neck.

"What do you feel?" she asked, her eyes closed and her mouth parted.

"You're so tense. So frustrated. There's a deep sense of longing inside of you."

"And you can tell that by just touching me?"

"That, and by the way you kissed me," he said.

"What are you going to do about it Night?" she asked. Night kissed her open lips, teasing her. She could feel his dick pressed against her stomach and it was just as impressive as the first time she'd felt it. He pulled away from her and Trinity almost wanted to cry out at the loss. But she let him go and watched as he went around to his desk.

"I'm very attracted to you Trinity. If that wasn't obvious," he said.

"And I wouldn't be here if I wasn't the least bit curious," Trinity replied, her brows quirking. She picked up her drink from the desk and took another gulp, starting to feel the effects. Night pulled out a sheet of paper from his desk drawer and a pen. He set the paper down with the pen on top of it and pushed it towards her.

"What is this?" she asked.

"Despite our attraction, you're still human. Past consequences have taught our kind to protect ourselves. That there is a contract. A contract that says you're allowing me to do any and everything sexually pleasing to your body within your discretion. I guess the only question is, are you bold enough to sign it?" Trinity locked eyes with Night. They were swirling with specs of gold and his fangs were elongating again. His stare was intense but he didn't hide behind a macho act.

"So, if I sign this contract, what are you going to do?" Trinity asked him.

"Kiss you," he shrugged.

"But you already kissed me without me having to sign this!" Trinity exclaimed.

"I'm talking about your other set of lips darling," he explained.

"You haven't lived until you've gotten your pussy sucked by a vampire," he stated, a dark sexy grin on his face, showing those perfectly sharpened fangs. Trinity gulped. She snatched up the contract quickly, scribbling her name across the dotted line as her heart drummed an exciting beat in her heart.

Chapter Nine

Trinity was clutching her drink tight as Night led her through a door at the back of his large office. She peered through the door first, seeing that it opened up to a corridor, dimly lit.

"You trust me?" Night asked her. Trinity swallowed and nodded.

"You've signed that contract, and I honor it by not harming you. Regardless of that, I would never hurt you Trinity. Do not fear me."

"I'm not afraid of you," she whispered. Maybe there was no fear because she'd seen a genuine part of him when he was dealing with that teenage vampire. He spoke like a leader and although he warned of a punishment, his demeanor wasn't evil or condescending. Trent couldn't even talk to her without being an asshole.

"That's good," he smiled.

"Wait a sec!" Trinity rushed back to his desk and grabbed the Hurricane that he didn't even sip. Hers was almost done and she was probably going to need a little bit more for whatever he had in store for her. Night only chuckled at her when she came back to stand next to him. He motioned for her to go first before he followed her into the corridor and closed the door. The hall was big enough for them to walk side by side. They walked by various doors on either side of the corridor, the carpet runner looking like something out of the 19th century.

"What are these doors?" Trinity asked.

"They lead to some of the rooms in the club so that way I can easily reach club level if anything goes wrong or if I'm needed," Night replied. They walked by a large black metal door that looked like something industrial.

"And that?" Trinity asked.

"It's to the basement of the club. Underneath the club is a bunker where some members of my clan live. Most of us have regular houses but others can't afford it so I've offered them the protection of the club to live rent free. I'm usually the only one that uses that door. Oh, and Blaze. The main entrance to the bunker is on club level."

"And no human has ever asked about it?"

"Humans see what they want to see. The door is in plain sight, but either they don't care or they've never taken the chance to look. Either way, it's none of their business," Night shrugged.

"Except for you. You can ask me anything you want," Night said, looking down at her with a wink. Trinity smiled before taking another sip. Nearly emptying her glass.

"Enough," Night declared, taking both glasses from her.

"Why?!" She whined.

"Because if you get too drunk to feel what my tongue will do to you, I'm gonna spank your ass raw darling," he said. Trinity gasped and grabbed her ass, already feeling the slaps he'd put on her. Truthfully, she wanted a spanking but that might have been the Hurricane talking.

"In here," he said, stopping at a door. He opened it for her and motioned for her to go in first. The room was large, equipped with a king size bed that was neatly made. The furniture was minimum but Trinity could smell Night's lingering scent.

"This is your room?" she asked.

"Yes. Most nights instead of going home I sleep here. Besides, when there's certain things going on, my clan feels better if their leader is in the same vicinity as them." Trinity went over to the bed and sat down on its pillow soft surface. Night placed their drinks on an accent table before opening what Trinity assumed was a closet door. He pulled out a chair complete with leather binds. Her eyes widened as she scooted off the bed and stood.

"What in the hell is this?" she asked.

"I made it. It's a prototype for our more daring rooms of the club. I haven't even tried it out yet, but I keep making changes and things. Tonight's the perfect night to see if it's ready, don't you think?" Trinity eyed the slim recliner that clearly could recline backwards but also had flaps where your calf would be strapped down to. There were binds attached to the flaps, the armrests and on each side of the padding for the headrest. It was an expensive looking chair, especially with the leather work. It meant Night was good with his hands. Trinity couldn't help but take that in a sexual context.

Moving swiftly towards her, Night wrapped his arm around her waist and tugged her towards his body.

"I don't know about that chair Night," Trinity breathed, his scent covering her completely, making her lose her mind. Night tilted her head up and kissed her mouth softly.

"You're gonna sit in my chair Trinity. And you're gonna like it," he replied. His kiss deepened, stealing her breath. Her body shivered as she kissed him wildly, the alcohol she'd consumed buzzing through her body and driving her lust. Night's hands moved down to her jean skirt and slowly untucked every button running down the center of it. The jean material fell to a heap on the ground, revealing the black lace thong. He reached around and cupped her ass, the plushness of it making Night groan as he kissed her deeply. Fuck. He'd never kissed a woman as deep since his beloved. Hell, he hadn't groped a woman like this since his beloved either. Her ass just felt so good in his hands. Her tongue felt so good in his mouth. Her body felt so good against his. The cool chestnut complexion of her skin, reddened under his palms that kneaded her pillows of a backside. His growing arousal became painful.

Night encompassed her in his arms, moving from her ass up her back and to her neck. He split their kiss for a second to yank her t-shirt over her head. Her bra accompanied her panties. Night pulled away from her completely. His eyes looked her up and down. Her body was fit, but she was oh so curvy, and her stomach dipped in the way a woman's stomach should. He didn't like women who wanted stomachs that matched his.

"What?" Trinity asked, crossing her arms over her stomach.

"Are vampire women more...fit?" she asked. Night made a face, his brows dipping. He pulled her close again and smacked his hand against her bottom.

"Ouch!" she yelped. He bit her ear, making sure she felt his fangs.

"When we're alone together, in a space of intimacy, don't mention other women. It's me and you. That's it." While he had her in his grasp, he unclasped her delicate bra and pulled it away. Her full breasts fell in front of him, heavy with her arousal. He kissed her again, pressing her breasts against his chest so he could feel their softness. While he kissed her, he walked backwards with her in his arms to his chair.

One moment Trinity was standing, the next moment her ass was in the plush leather chair. Night worked fast, almost too fast for her to track as her wrists were strapped down by the binds. Her chest rose up and down rapidly as she watched him bind her ankles to the flaps of the chair.

"Easy darling," he said, pressing a warm hand on her stomach. Trinity took a deep breath to relax herself. Night leaned over her, hovering just inches from her lips that he'd kissed pink. Trinity thought he was going to kiss her again until her chair flopped back, setting her in a reclined position. He chuckled at her reaction as he moved towards her legs. He raised the flaps that her legs were strapped down on and pushed them to the sides, making Trinity's legs open wide.

"How flexible are you?" Night asked her, continuing to push the flaps, realizing that Trinity's legs almost made a horizontal line at how wide she could tolerate them being open.

"Flexible enough," she managed to answer. Night adjusted the height of the chair. He sat right in front of her opened legs and made sure the chair was at the perfect height to allow his mouth to feast on his prize.

"Oh god," Trinity breathed.

"What? I didn't even do anything yet,"

"The anticipation is killing me," she heaved. She tried to hump her hips forward so she could feel his mouth on her, but it didn't work. Not while she was strapped down like this. Night grinned. He sensed her misery so he quickly put her out of it. She was still wearing her thong but he wasn't ready to take it off yet. Through the black lace, he saw her yearning pink bud that was already producing sweet juices. Night wanted a taste.

With the tip of his tongue, he drew a circle around her growing bud. The fabric of the lace was the rough texture her clit needed to have her hips jerking.

"Oh. That's different," Trinity breathed. Night continued to swirl his tongue along her clit, gaining soft moans from her lips. The flat of his tongue rubbed against the underside of her clit, making sure the lace followed his tongue movement. Trinity looked down at Night, watching his tongue do the work. Her hips continued to jerk, and where she would have moved away if she was in a normal position, she found it wasn't possible now. Her insides were squeezing with her impending release, his work on her clit too good and too consistent to delay her release. She tossed her head back as her legs trembled. She came hard, her whole-body twitching as she tried to fight the binds. Night pulled her entire clit into his mouth along with the fabric and teased her clit between his lips.

"Oh, you muthafucking vamp," she cried out, as she came again, the second orgasm plowing through her like a football player.

"Easy now," Night said softly when he released her aching clit. He patted it softy, making her shiver again.

"That was very good. I'm very satisfied," Trinity said as she tried to catch her breath. Night looked up at her.

"I am not done yet darling," he said. He held up an index finger, letting his nail elongate into a sharp claw. He drew his nail over her thong, ripping the fabric. With it ripped, he let his fingernail retreat and then he simply pulled the material off her body.

"Not done?" Trinity asked.

"Did you really think I put you in this contraption to suck your pussy for 2 minutes? You disappoint me darling," Night said, shaking his head. Before Trinity could protest, Night's tongue speared through her, no barrier of the lace between them now. Trinity felt her eyes rolling to the back of her head as his entire tongue swirled around her insides.

"Hmm, Trinity. You taste amazing," he growled, sending vibrations through her most sensitive parts. His lips sucked at her clit while his tongue rolled against it. He pulled it taut, savoring her taste before letting her pop out of his mouth. Trinity felt herself gushing, juices just exploding out of her.

"Wait, Night—ugh, I'm about to-" Trinity let out a high-pitched scream as she came again, this time harder than the first two. Night was growling as he swallowed the juices that came squirting out of her. Vampires didn't have the ability to get drunk but Night felt intoxicated as he drank her juices. Her taste was fresh with a hint of honey.

"Please, un—untie me," Trinity begged, trying to jerk her hips away from Night's assaulting tongue. Her body shook as he slowly swirled his tongue around her opening. She thought he was going to go right back in for the kill but he finally backed away. Trinity sighed and let her head fall back. Emma was not joking when she said vampires ate like their lives depended on it.

"Feeling good darling?" Night asked her, running his hands up her body.

"I can use a drink," she said, pushing her chin out to the Hurricane.

"I'll give you a drink soon," Night assured her. He stood as he trailed his hands up her stomach, towards her breasts. While he gave her pussy a little break, he still wanted to feast on her. He leaned down and pulled her nipple into his mouth.

For some reason, Trinity thought he was going to be as rough as Trent had been but no. Night was tender as he rolled her nipple around in his mouth and sucked it softly. His hands kneaded her mounds in a caressing manner. Trinity had never moaned from her breasts being touched or sucked, but here she was, moaning something serious for Night. Her hips began jerking upwards again, eager to feel something inside of her.

"Looks like my little honeypot is ready," Night said, popping her breast from his mouth. He placed his hand under her left leg and began to raise it up. Trinity's eyes widened as he reached over and did the same to her right leg. Her hips slightly bent in the chair as he raised both her legs, her feet pointing to the ceiling. He kept them stretched apart, creating a 'V', but slightly wider. He adjusted the height on the chair, raising it so he could stay standing, even though he had to lean over a little bit. No words were exchanged between them as Night settled between her legs again, leaning over her. He adjusted her legs, opening them wider so her clit was poking out. He went back to using his tip, drawing circles around her clit again, this time there was no fabric between them.

"Whoa!" Trinity gasped, trying to hump her hips upwards to apply more pressure from his tongue. But Night retained the pressure, using the tip of his tongue in slow lazy circles. Her insides were tightening again and releasing, aching for something more, needing something more. His tongue moved to tight jerky movements that began to squeeze an orgasm out of her. just as she reached her peak, his tongue slowed again.

"No! Don't stop that! Oh, the minute you untie me Night, I'm gonna fuck you-" He dipped his tongue inside of her tightening opening and fucked her with his tongue. He pinched her clit and Trinity was erupting again. Night went between sucking her pussy and fucking her pussy with his tongue. She felt her legs moving backwards as Night stood between them, pushing at the underside of her thighs, bringing her legs closer to her chest. Standing, he had enough leverage to stroke her with his tongue evenly, dipping his head up and down. Trinity craned her neck to look down at what he was doing, astonished that his tongue was giving it to her better than Trent's dick had. She was moaning in a way she hadn't ever before, the restriction of her limbs making her orgasm even more magnificent. His tongue swooped out of her insides and swirled all over her leaking lips, the sound of his lips sucking and slopping, echoing off the walls in the room. While his tongue did the work, he pushed two fingers inside of her, pressing at her g-spot.

Trinity screamed as she squirted a jet stream straight into the air. She fought the binds hard, her body wanting to curl in on itself as she orgasmed. The veins in her neck were plump as she screamed out, the power of the orgasm forcing tears from her eyes.

"Night! Night! Night!" Trinity screamed, unable to say anything else.

"Please! I can't—I can't take it anymore," she cried out, tossing her head from side to side. Night was still sucking her pussy, his tongue stroking at the underside of her clit again, making Trinity come nonstop. He wrapped his lips around her clit and suckled, the vibrations throwing Trinity into insanity.

One second his warm tongue was digging her out, and the next second, her entire pussy was drowning in the cold liquid of the untouched Hurricane. Trinity craned her neck, her mouth wide open as she watched Night slowly pour the Hurricane over her pussy, making sure the stream landed directly on the clit first. The steady stream sparked another orgasm like the ones you had when you used the showerhead in the tub. The slim ice chips numbed her pussy lips but at the same time felt so fucking good. Her hips began humping again, unable to stop coming.

Night drained the glass, then topped off her clit with the cherry that had garnished the drink. He winked at her as he leaned down and swiped his warm tongue over her pussy lips. He captured the cherry in his mouth, but used it to dive back in between her lips, slurping at her once more. As she screamed in ecstasy, she felt the chair reclining backwards again, moving until she was nearly upside down. Night stood at full height, not having to lean over as her pussy was higher with her lower half nearly touching the ground. He dug deeper and deeper, sucking as if he was trying to pull her uterus straight from her body. Trinity's body just went limp, unable to fight, unable to run away from the endless orgasms. Her voice was scratchy as she kept moaning, crying and begging for him to stop.

Finally eating the cherry, Night swiped up her pussy again as if he was cleaning her like feline shifters would do. Moving to the right slightly, he licked the inside of her thigh before he slowly bit into the ripe vein close to her pussy. Her blood was wild and fragrant, and hit Night in the stomach like a powerful punch. He gripped the chair, the leather cracking under the strength of his grasp as he tried to control that savage deep inside him that went crazy at the taste of Trinity's blood. He felt his veins open up and accepted her as the perfect meal. His lungs clenched as if he couldn't breathe, Trinity's essence just knocking him breathless. Her essence wasn't just filling his need to feed however. It trickled through to his heart, slowly wrapping itself around his most vital organ. Night closed his eyes as he sucked softly. Her pussy streamed more juices out of her, the bite extracting another orgasm.

The bite wasn't anything like Trinity expected. There was a slight pinch, and she felt his teeth enter her body, but the moment he began to suck, her lower muscles tightened and then she was rolling on another orgasm. She felt as if she'd smoked 5 blunts back to back, the bite making her high and delusional with pleasure. She was floating, her pussy squirting and twitching. He drank slowly before extracting his teeth and licking the bite wound closed. When he looked at her pussy, her lips were quivering, just begging him for more. His dick was beyond hard, painfully restricted behind his jeans. His mind cloudy with raging arousal, Night fumbled with his jeans, unbuttoning them. Trinity craned her neck up, trying to see what he was doing. She drew in a sharp gasp when his length, thick and stiff sprang from his jeans. His dark flesh matched his deep complexion. He hung so thick Trinity feared her insides.

"I can't catch human diseases, and my sperm will not impregnate you unless you're a vampire," Night breathed. He dragged the chair closer to the bed so he could use the foot frame as leverage.

"Fuck, just put it in Night!" Trinity cried desperately, needing to feel him inside of her. Night tilted the chair back all the way, putting her head on the ground. He levered himself, placing his tip at her entrance. With her legs bound down and stretched open, Trinity could look up from where she laid on the floor to see him penetrating her. She'd never tried any position like this that had her feet in the air, with her head touching the ground, but Night had gotten her in this position.

He tapped her clit, making her eyes cross from the pleasure. He slowly began to slide in, his thick head spearing her lips apart. Her muscles were already contracting, waiting to gobble him up. She was well lubricated so he slid in easily but not without burn from his size. He stretched her so effortlessly, Trinity was already on the edge of an orgasm, her eyes snapped shut. He didn't stop midway like Trent. He pierced her insides completely, embedding himself into her womb, deep in her guts. Trinity wished she could hold onto him as they became one. He pulled out slowly and slammed home, jerking his hips forward so it bumped against her clit. He pulled out a second time and again, slammed inside of her. Trinity's stomach imploded. She tried to hang onto his dick with her muscles, but the leakage of her orgasm produced too much lubricant for her to continue holding on.

"Night, wait! Don't!" Trinity screamed, wanting him to pause his strokes to give her a moment to recuperate but it was too late. His thick dick eased in and out of her with the right amount of pressure until she burst completely open.

As Trinity orgasmed, Night tried his hardest to hide the savage inside of him. The last thing he wanted to do was scare her while she was in the throes of passion. His nails elongated and scraped against the wooden foot board. His eyes were beginning to burn amber, and slowly turn to orange as he continued to plunge inside of her. His fangs were heavy and aching, needing to feel the flesh of her neck in his mouth, her blood coating his tongue. But he knew it wouldn't be a simple feeding. The small part of her that had wrapped around his heart thumped hard, becoming bright inside of his body. If he bit her, he was going to change her. He was going to need to change her.

"Oh my god, oh god, oh fuck!" The words tumbled out of

her mouth as her head began moving from side to side in her uncontrolled orgasm. A growl from deep within him, rumbled out and began a shout as Night fought that desperate urge to make her one with him completely. He came hard, his back feeling like it was breaking as he slammed into her, and emptied his seed into her guts. Trinity's body was seizing slightly, as her eyes were rolling in her head. He felt her insides fluttering and squeezing him in her repeated orgasms. As her flutters slowed down, Night slowly pulled out of her, loving the way his dark skin looked against her hazelnut complexion, with her pink lips still trying to grip at him. He popped out of her. *Slosh.* His dick fell wetly against her clit. *Slop.*

Trinity's chest was heaving up and down as she tried to catch her breath. Fearing she was uncomfortable; Night slowly set the chair upright and lowered her legs. She looked at him with glazed over eyes, watching as he unbound her. When she was free, her body fell forward as if she had no control of her limbs. Night grabbed her.

"Darling?" he asked her. Trinity just made a sound in her throat, her body floppy in his arms.

"How? How—so good? But how?" she mumbled, talking to herself. Night chuckled as he carried her to his bed. He set her down softly, pushing her coils from her face. A smile touched her lips when she looked at him, their gazes locking. Night felt that thump again and the flare of her essence that was wrapped around his heart, tightening. He didn't know why he'd ever dreamed about Trinity in the first place, but as of that moment, he figured it out very quickly.

Chapter Ten

TRINITY DIDN'T KNOW WHEN SHE'D FALLEN ASLEEP, BUT when she registered consciousness again, Night wasn't next to her. She blinked and looked around the dark room, moonlight streaming through the gray curtains against the windows. At least the sun wasn't coming up. That would have meant Trinity was at the club all night. She wasn't sure if any excuse she came up with, Trent would listen to. Then again, Trinity didn't even care. When she stretched, her bones cracked and the dull ache between her legs made her smile. This was going to be a night to remember for sure. Trinity just couldn't believe she'd been with a vampire. And it was beyond everything she expected. She looked between her legs where he'd bitten her, but there was no bite mark. Then she realized she was full dressed, and she felt as if she was cleaned. Instead of the clothes she'd worn to the club however, she was dressed in a black slip with spaghetti straps. It smelled of Night.

"Wait," Trinity pressed her arm to her nose and inhaled. It wasn't the dress that smelled of Night. *She* smelled liked Night. There was a funny feeling inside of her that told her a simple shower wouldn't take his scent off of her skin. It felt as if his scent was permanently there. Oddly enough, Trinity didn't care.

She scooted out of the bed, rising slowly to test her legs. When she was stable; she tip-toed out of the room and followed the corridor the way Night had brought her in. When she peeked into his office, he was sitting at his desk, with his cell-phone to his ear.

"Is he okay?" Night was asking whoever he was on the phone with. He paused and listened to the person speak.

"I don't want you to worry about this Eline, I will protect your son should things get out of hand. But please, advise your son not to try and retaliate it will only make things worse. Me and my clan protectors will find the people responsible for this and make sure they are held accountable." He said a few more words before he finally hung up the phone. Trinity was still standing in the doorway and she hadn't made a sound but the moment he ended his call, he turned and looked directly at her.

"Rise and shine," he smiled.

"Who was that on the phone?" Trinity asked, her curiosity getting the better of her.

"A mother was concerned that her son was going to get into some trouble with the human law," Night replied.

"What happened?"

"A human tried to drive a stake through his heart."

"Why would someone do that?!" Trinity gasped.

"Because they probably thought it was funny," Night shrugged. Trinity realized how difficult it must have been for vampires to just exist when humans did stupid things like that.

"I'm sorry, Night," she apologized.

"Don't be darling. You don't have to apologize for their stupidity," Night assured her. He motioned for her to come to him. Trinity didn't hesitate. She walked to his desk as he rolled his chair back. He pulled her hand softly and brought her behind his desk and plopped her down on his lap. She sat comfortably as he rolled back closer to the desk where he had paperwork in neat piles. Leaning against his chest and watching him scribble his signature on various sheets of paper was very relaxing to her. Being in is arms, against him, it just felt *right*.

"Wait a minute. Don't I owe you some money?" Trinity asked when she saw him looking at a check someone had sent to the club. The heading was entitled 'Goods and Services'. It reminded Trinity that they'd had sex and Emma had said, to fuck a vampire, you'd have to pay them. That's just the way the club works.

"Pardon?" he asked her, turning his head to look at her with a thick arched brow.

"We ended up with your dick inside me. Emma said that means the human has to pay-"

"No—no—no," Night said, waving her off.

"Your friend was correct Trinity, but I did not have sex with you for monetary purposes. Either way, those are the rules of the club. Technically, we did not fuck in the club." Night flashed her a smile. Her heart began to thump wildly again. This time it felt different. As if something was tightening around her heart. She felt as if she could feel Night's very spirit within her. But even that thought was insane. She didn't truly know this man.

"Then I think you owe me money. Didn't you drink my blood? Trinity asked with a teasing smile.

"Name your price," Night replied with a matching grin on his face. Even though she had no money of her own, and she could easily use money from Night to shed the weight of her parents, it wouldn't solve her problems. Plus, she didn't come to him this night for anything of monetary value either.

"Keep your money Dracula," she laughed. Night's brows quirked.

"Oh, that's so funny! Like I haven't heard that one before,"

Night said sarcastically. Trinity chuckled as she tried to rise from his lap. Night kept his arm around her firmly, his eyes flashing that deep amber color. He clearly did not want to let her go.

"Where you going?" he asked.

"I have to go find Emma. Plus, I can't stay here all night, I have to go home," she replied.

"Oh," Night said, his arm starting to loosen a little bit. The expression on his face looked as if he felt silly.

"It's alright. You don't have to feel bad. I don't want to leave either, but I kind of have to. I'll come back to you tomorrow, I won't just abandon you, Night," she told him, as if she could read his mind and his emotions. In a way, she felt as if she could. His eyes started to glow amber again.

"You could tell that's what I was feeling?" he asked. Trinity just nodded, taking one of his locks from his shoulder and twirling it in her hand.

"How come your eyes glow like that and then go back to deep brown?" she asked.

"In moments where my heart rate spikes immensely, or when I experience an imbalance of emotion, they begin to change. This happens to all vampires. It's just in our nature," he answered her.

"I like both your eye colors. They're mesmerizing."

"You're mesmerizing," Night countered, running his thumb across her bottom lip.

"I meant what I said. I'll come back tomorrow. I'll even give you my phone number." She picked up his phone from the desk and quickly typed in her number and saved it. Night felt satisfied at having a way to easily reach her, even though with her essence in every beat of his heart, he knew he'd always be able to find her now. The fact that she could tell what he was feeling meant that he wasn't the only one feeling the effects of what had taken place in his bedroom.

"I'll help you look for your friend," Night said. He began to stand, keeping an arm around her waist as he stood completely, and then set her dangling feet on the ground. When he didn't remove his arm from around her, Trinity understood that he wanted to walk with her closer to him. If this were Trent, she would have a problem. Night though? Oh, he could hold onto her all damn night.

Walking down from the second floor where his office was located, Trinity and Night joined the dark club, flashing with colorful lights. The air was stuffier on club level because of all the heated bodies, grinding and rubbing against each other. Trinity didn't realize how popular her vamp was until he showed his face on club level. Several people called out to him, wanting his attention. As they stood next to the bar, a woman came up to Night quickly. She began jabbering off at the mouth, talking about some problem with the human men that came to the club. Night listened aptly, nodding. His arm came from around Trinity's waist as he continued to talk to the woman. While he wasn't holding her, Trinity began to slowly drift away, taking in the sights of the club. It was large and spacious, the center of the club a dancefloor that was writhing with grinding bodies. The booths against each wall were dedicated to feeding but from what Trinity saw, even on the dancefloor, vampires were drinking blood from their human hosts. On the far-left side of the club, three archways led to dark corridors that Trinity could guess were where those special rooms were for humans who wanted more than just a bite from a vampire.

Looking back, Trinity saw that Night was still in deep conversation with the woman who'd approached him, so she kept drifting, her nosiness taking over. She inched by all the bodies, staying out of the way and out of sight, trying not to disturb anyone who was deep into their pleasures.

A woman slid by Trinity, catching her attention immediately. She didn't see the woman's face, or heard the woman even speak, but there was something familiar about the outline of the woman as she walked through the club. Trinity followed her, unable to help herself. The woman's hair was long, the black tresses splaying down her back in the revealing dress she wore. She went deeper into the crowd. Trinity realized the woman must have been meeting someone. She was looking all around until a vampire appeared in front of her and scooped her up, sliding his hands beneath her thighs and hiking her up so her legs wrapped around his waist. Her dress lifted, showing the lingerie she had on underneath, but the woman didn't care. The vampire carried her off, already sliding his teeth into her neck. Trinity followed still, her curiosity now at its top peak.

The vampire carried the woman off quickly, making it hard for Trinity to make out the woman's face. She kept up as best as she could, sliding through the crowd as the vampire went towards the archways that led to the corridors. As if they were too eager to get to a bedroom, the vampire was already sliding down his pants, Trinity could see the mounds of his bare ass. He leaned the woman against the wall, next to the archway and his hips jutted forward, signaling that he had just entered her forcefully. A strobe light crossed the woman's face whose eyes were closed as ecstasy painted her features. Trinity gasped. Now she realized why she had to follow the woman who she swore she knew. Trinity backed away quickly before turning around sharply. She bumped right into Night's chest.

"There you are. Don't run off from me like that again," he scolded.

"Sorry," Trinity smiled.

"Are you alright? Your heart is racing."

"Oh no, I'm fine," Trinity lied. Night looked at her suspiciously, the strobe lights crossing over his face, but he didn't argue with her.

"I found your friend," he said, taking her hand. He guided

her through the crowd that seemingly just parted as he walked by. He didn't have to snake around people to get to where he was going. That was a man in charge.

Emma was waiting at the bar with Blaze next to her, grinning from ear to ear. Even though Trinity felt just as happy at what she'd done with Night, what she'd just saw shocked her too her core.

"Let's go," she said to Emma, taking her hand. She dragged Emma out of the club with Night and Blaze following them. They headed around back where Trinity had parked the mustang.

"Well damn, you're in a rush. Was it that bad? Did you not like having your blood sucked?" Emma asked. Trinity turned around and gave Emma a look.

"What? No! I fucking loved it," Trinity said, looking at Night.

"You better had," he grunted. Trinity stuck her tongue out at him even as she tried not to smile.

"So then what's the rush?" Emma asked.

"I just have to get home," Trinity replied, giving Emma a low look. Emma immediately realized the problem.

"Right! Home. Yeah, we should probably go," Emma said, looking at the two men. Blaze leaned in and sniffed Trinity. Trinity smacked at his chest.

"Boy, if you don't back up!" Trinity snapped at him.

"Stop it. Don't smell her," Night scolded, yanking Blaze away from Trinity.

"Sorry! You just smell...different. My apologies." Blaze said. He looked at Night who just grunted.

"And here I was thinking I was special," Emma said, crossing her arms. Blaze finally saw the pout on her face.

"Oh no, my sweet Emma, you are definitely special. Me smelling Trinity was not at all in any way besides curiosity.

Believe me my sweet," Blaze said, reaching out to capture her in his arms. He kissed her lips tenderly.

"And just like that, you're forgiven," Emma smiled.

"Now, me and Trinity have to get going alright," Emma said, backing up towards Trinity.

"Don't disappear on me Trinity," Night said.

"I told you I wouldn't Night. I promise." She rushed into his embrace, hugging him tightly. She rose on her tip-toes and kissed him deeply, feeling her heart pump wild. Emma literally had to peel Trinity away from Night to get her off the man. Even as she moved towards the mustang, she walked backwards, so she could look at Night for as long as she could. When she finally had to disappear into the car, she blew him a kiss.

"She's special, isn't she?" Blaze asked Night.

"Whatever do you mean?" Night asked, feeling his heart sink at watching Trinity driving away in that mustang. He felt as if he was losing part of himself.

"You scent marked her. Any vampire that comes near her is gonna know she belongs to you. And you don't just scent mark females you drink blood from. So, this means she's special. It has to be," Blaze explained. Night crossed his arms and took several deep breaths, still looking out at the mustang, seeing the taillights in the distance.

"She's my true mate," Night grunted before he turned and walked off, leaving Blaze behind. All Night could think about was how he was going to sleep for the rest of the night without having Trinity in his arms.

TRINITY FELT like a puppy whose owner just left them for the day. She kept looking in her rearview mirror expecting Night to be running after the car, calling out to her. Not even five minutes had passed by, but she felt a horrible sinking in her chest at being away from him. She wanted his touch, wanted to feel his heat.

"That was a steamy ass kiss," Emma giggled. "Had a good night then?"

"It was amazing. He set me up in this chair and sucked my pussy until I cried. Then he stuffed his dick in me and I came after only three strokes. Girl, my pussy is still sore," Trinity said. Emma gasped.

"You actually had sex with him?"

"Oh yeah. He didn't charge me though. He said it wasn't about money. He sucked my blood and it made me orgasm even more, but I didn't take any money from him."

"Why?"

"I don't know. I just feel...a connection with him. It's hard to explain. But I am coming back to this club tomorrow because I'm officially addicted."

"Girl, I told you," Emma laughed. Her laughter died out slowly.

"Wait, if you're already addicted why'd you wanna leave so quick? I know you could care less about getting home to Trent or doing shit to please Trent. What's the rush?" Emma asked.

"I saw someone at the club. Getting fucked up against the wall by a vampire while they drank her blood," Trinity said.

"Who?" Emma questioned. Trinity clenched the steering wheel, still in shock about what she'd seen. She actually didn't know if it was shock or something else. She just really couldn't fathom this reality.

"My mother," Trinity revealed.

Chapter Eleven

TRINITY WAS STARTLED AWAKE BY INTENSE BANGING ON Trent's guest room door. She groaned and muttered curses.

"Go the fuck away!" Trinity snapped. She'd just fallen asleep as the sun came up, restless from the events of the past night.

"Get your ass up! I have some important people coming in the hour. I would like my fiancée to be present. Get up. Get dressed." He shouted through the door. Trinity grunted hard. She rolled over and threw a mini tantrum. She threw her pillows, cursing loudly as she finally got out of the bed.

"This is some bullshit," she groaned as she shuffled to the bathroom. She turned on the shower, and began stripping from her night clothes as the water warmed up. Her body was still humming from Night's touch and her mind racing from the fact that she'd seen her mother at the very club she told Trinity to stay away from. Even though her mother was a clear hypocrite, Trinity wished she could have woken up in Night's arms instead of this place. Now, she had to pretend she gave a damn about being Trent's fiancée and playing her dutiful role in front of company. The night before had changed her. She felt something deep inside her was different and no matter what happened from now on, those events at the club were going to be part of her. But how could she use what she'd discovered about her mother to her advantage?

In the shower, Trinity's bones melded and relaxed even though the space between her thighs continued to hum. When Trinity closed her eyes, she could feel Night's thick length stroking in and out of her with intensity. Her knees began to shake, a heavy arousal rising through her body. Her nipples hardened as her breasts felt heavy against her chest. Unable to help herself, Trinity slid her hands down her body and slipped a finger in between her hot slick folds. A soft moan escaped her mouth. She could still feel the way Night's tongue had treated her and in that moment she craved more. To be sucked by a vampire; it was like something straight from hell. Hot and forbidden.

"I hope you're getting dressed!" Trent was banging on the bedroom door again snapping Trinity from her heated thoughts. She was thankful she had locked the guest room door or else Trent would have been barging inside and invading her space. She growled and finished her shower quickly, wetting her hair to reactivate the product on her tresses and renew her curls. She shook her hair out before cutting off the water and stepping out of the shower. She dried herself lazily before she began blow drying her curls to give it a wash and go effect.

Once her hair was completely dry, she brushed her teeth and washed her face before simply applying toner and moisturizer. She plumped her lips with shiny lip gloss then left the bathroom. She wanted to just wear a t-shirt with no bra and biker shorts but Trent would not let her live if she did. So instead, she dressed in a plaid patterned sundress and red classic heels to match. After putting in small gold hooped earrings, and spraying her neck with perfume, she left the bedroom. She jumped in surprise when she bumped right into Trent who was pacing in front of the door. He was dressed in khaki's and a button-down shirt and loafers. He looked her up and down and Trinity just knew he was evaluating her.

"You look amazing Trinity," he said, leaning down to kiss her. Trinity moved her head to the side slightly so he lips fell on her jawline instead of her lips. He grunted in disapproval but didn't say anything about it.

"Didn't you have a meeting? And who are these people?" Trinity asked.

"I had my meeting early morning Trinity. It's after 10am now. I let you do as you please but staying out late like you did last night is a no-no. You will not be doing it again," he said.

"Try and stop me," Trinity dared. He could only just glare at her.

"Our guests are downstairs. I told them you're just preparing some things for the wedding is why you're tardy. Now, you look amazing Trinity but I need you to change your hair," he said.

"Change my hair?" Trinity asked.

"Yes. Go and straighten it," he ordered.

"I thought my afro looked pretty damn good," she said, fluffing her curls.

"It does Trinity. It's amazing. But it's not appropriate for who we are. Go do what I said." Trinity crossed her arms and leaned against the door.

"I'm not changing my hair Trent," she said softly.

"Then you cannot be part of this gathering. I will not have a fiancée not looking the proper part. If you keep this up Trinity, your parents are going to suffer a severe cost if you keep pulling shit like this," he threatened. Trinity rolled her eyes.

"Go fuck yourself," she stated softly. She walked off, making sure that as she turned, her curls smacked him in the face. She went back into the bedroom and snatched off her dress, tugging at it angrily. Tears were brimming her eyes as she changed into another cropped t-shirt, and jean shorts. She shoved her feet in black flip flips and snatched up her purse. Trent was nowhere to be found when she left the bedroom but she didn't care. She walked down the hall and snuck out of the house through the backdoor next to the kitchen. Since she still had the mustang keys, she hopped in the car and drove off in it, heading to her parent's home.

"What a nice surprise! I thought you'd be enjoying your time with your new fiancé," her father greeted her. Trinity only scoffed and pushed through the front door, entering the house.

"Oh no. I know that look. What did you do Trinity?" he asked.

"I didn't do anything! I dressed up all pretty and nice for his fucking guests that I could give a damn about, and he tells me that my hair is not appropriate and I needed to straighten it! I mean come on! I'm already pretending that I wanna be part of this rich stuck up ass family, engaged to the jerk of Louisiana, and now I have to pretend that I'm not black? That my hair isn't kinky coils and defies gravity? I straighten my hair for your galas and parties but I refuse to wear straight hair every day to fit some damn image. It's not me. and I refuse to pretend anymore," Trinity huffed out.

"I can't believe this. All this extra attitude over something as simple as hair? Trinity if you straighten your hair it will eventually go back to being curly! You need to learn to sacrifice for once. Everything isn't all about you," her father scolded. Trinity just looked at him, wondering what would happen if she drew her hand back and smacked fire out of her own father.

"I don't know why you expect anything better out of her," Tracee said, coming towards them.

"Daddy, why don't I go over Trent's and try to smooth things over. No doubt he's probably feeling rejected with his company because little miss spoiled wanted to have her own way," Tracee offered.

"That's a good idea sweetie. And tell him, me and your

mother are dealing with Trinity, and it won't happen again," James said. Trinity watched as her sister left the house. She was already dressed in a knee length pink dress and her hair was straightened, falling down her shoulders. She didn't care that her sister was going to clean up her so called mess, but she cared that no one seemed to realize how much Trinity was sacrificing. Her happiness was one of those things.

"Now come. Let's have a chat," James scolded. He took Trinity by the elbow and led her to the day room where her mother was sitting on the couch, sipping a cup of tea. She had a faint smile at the corners of her mouth and something about that just made Trinity's blood boil.

"Oh, my child! I didn't expect to see you here. Is something wrong?" Rose asked.

"Trent wanted her hair straightened and she threw a fit," James informed his wife.

"Trinity, you've got to learn to be an obedient wife. It may be rough at first, but trust me, it'll work better in your favor. Ask your father, we gel so well because I learned to listen. Once I learned to listen, he made sure to take care of my wants and needs no matter what they were. Trent will do the same for you." Trinity sat on the chair across from the sofa her mother was sitting in, with her feet tucked up under her. Trinity crossed her legs.

"Wants and needs huh?" Trinity asked.

"Yes. I am always satisfied. That's what a good marriage does to you."

"Well in that case, what were you two doing last night? Surely as happily married as you are, the two of you were probably doing it like monkeys all night huh?" Trinity said. Her mother chuckled nervously.

"Believe it or not, but me and your mother share a very healthy sexual relationship. We're not that old after all. But we weren't doing anything like monkeys."

"Oh? So then what were you two doing?" Trinity asked. Then she looked at her mother.

"What did you do last night mother?" Trinity asked her mother specifically. Rose sipped her tea, the hand holding her teacup shaking slightly.

"I had a slight headache so I took some medicine and went to bed. Your father was a good husband and left me alone in my spare bedroom to rest. He knows I can be quite evil when I don't feel well," she responded. Even her words were shaky.

"Father, can I speak with mother alone? These problems I have with Trent, only mother can really help me. Being a woman and all," Trinity said.

"Of course! I'll be in my office setting up some tea times with a few people." James leaned down and kissed Trinity on the forehead before kissing his wife on the lips softly. Trinity glared at her mother, listening as her father's footsteps sounded further and further away.

"That's what you did last night?" Trinity asked.

"Yes. You know I always get horrible headaches." Trinity crossed her arms.

"You're lying," Trinity shrugged.

"Excuse me?!" Rose exclaimed.

"You're a liar."

"I don't know what's wrong with you, but I will not tolerate being spoken to like that! I am your mother and you will respect me!" she snapped.

"Alright, I apologize," Trinity said. Rose nodded.

"Just answer me this mother. Did you have a headache before or after you got fucked by that vampire?" Trinity asked. Rose's shaking was uncontrollable this time. She set her teacup down and glared at her daughter.

"Now. I don't know how you know this, but you'd better keep your damn mouth shut!" Rose was breathing heavy as she looked at Trinity.

"I can't believe you," Trinity said shaking her head.

"Here I am, unhappy as hell and you know I am, yet still you're telling me to be obedient and it'll all get better. To continue to act like something I'm not and eventually it'll turn out good. Giving me all these lectures about happiness and being a good wife, when you're at a vampire club getting your kicks off with a vampire. And I saw your face mother. You were enjoying it. The way you were with him, it wasn't your first time at that club. So tell me. Why should I sit here and act like I want anything to do with Trent when you're here having your own fun and doing what you want? Huh?" Trinity asked.

"Because this is our way of life. Me and your father signed a contract. Whether you want to or not, you've gotta marry Trent and that's just that. Obviously, you were at the club to get your own damn kicks off, so don't turn your nose up at me. The difference between you and I? I do what I need to do in front of the public. I am a mother and a wife and I play my part. But on my own time, in the darkness of night, I do what I want. But I know how to keep a damn secret. You're gonna marry Trent and act the way you need to Trinity, and you can fulfill your every desire with whomever you want as long as you know the way to act when the time is right."

"And you think that's okay? Cheating on dad? Being fucked by vampires and then coming home to your husband like you're the perfect wife?" Trinity asked.

"Ha. Don't think your father is so innocent child," Rose muttered.

"This family is full of liars and hypocrites," Trinity stated. She stood slowly and looked down at her mother, letting their eyes connect. She saw that her mother was not the least bit shamed in her actions. Trinity could only shake her head and leave. She was done following her family's rules. She rushed out of her parent's home, jumping back into the mustang to drive out of the large gates. She was gripping the steering wheel tightly, a scream of frustration threatening to leave her throat.

A motorcycle came barreling towards her on the opposite side of the street. It crossed in front of her, entering her lane. Trinity pressed on the brakes and turned her wheel, trying to careen in a different direction before she hit the motorist.

"What are you doing?! Are you drunk?!" Trinity screamed, as she rolled down her window. The man on the bike whipped off his black helmet. Thick locks spanned down his back and against his face. Dark eyes resembling dark chocolate glared at her through the car window.

"Night," Trinity gasped. He continued to glare at her, his thick brows furrowed and his chest rising and falling. Despite the expression on his face, Trinity suddenly felt deep waves of anger and jealousy searing through him. Something had riled him up immensely for him to even dare to leave vamp town in daylight to come find her.

Chapter Twelve

"I STILL DON'T UNDERSTAND HOW YOU COULD HAVE JUST let her leave," Blaze said, watching as Night ate his breakfast calmly. Ever since Night had dropped the M bomb, Blaze had been flipping out, excited and eager for his oldest friend to finally have found another woman that would steal his heart again.

"Because she doesn't understand our world. And I wasn't going to keep her here against her will," Night replied.

"It wouldn't be against her will. She would have wanted to stay."

"Obviously, you saw that she had to leave," Night said.

"Listen to me. You had better not push her away. Not after all the heartache you've felt." Night leaned back in his chair.

"I'm not going to push her away Blaze. I fully intend to have her in my life," Night said confidently. Blaze sighed in relief, believing his friend. He wasn't attempting to act like Trinity didn't belong to him.

"What are you gonna do now?" Blaze asked. Night pushed his tray of food away.

"I wonder what she's all about. Humans now, they post everything about themselves on the internet for people to find."

Blaze said. He stood from the couch and went over to Night's desk, pulling a chair behind it. He powered up Night's laptop and opened the web browser.

"I don't understand. Don't they know nothing about privacy?" Night asked.

"Apparently it's okay for them to tell all their business on the internet, but if the police invade their privacy they get real mad. Human thing I guess." Blaze shrugged as he searched the internet. He pulled up various social media pages but couldn't find anything about their Trinity. They didn't even know her last name.

"Just Google her name," Night suggested. Blaze closed out social media and typed her name in through google. It turned up way too many results so Blaze tried to limit it by typing in her name again along with Louisiana and family. A photo came up of Trinity with the rest of her family.

"Well, well, well, look at this. She's one of those rich ones who loves to turn their noses up at us after they get their pleasure from us," Blaze said, scrolling along all the pictures. Night leaned forward and looked at the photos. In all of them he saw the same thing from Trinity. She was smiling, but she wasn't happy. Every single photo taken was a forced pose. Immediately, Night began to feel sorry for his little mate, for having to be forced into a lifestyle that wasn't hers. She was miserable.

"Oh shit," Blaze gasped.

"What?" Night asked, looking at the computer. He pulled up a photo of Trinity wearing a beautiful gown standing next to a man who had his arm around her waist. The photo was candid so Trinity wasn't looking at the photographer but the caption was: 'Finally Engaged'.

"When was that taken?" Night asked, his voice going low.

"Very recent," Blaze admitted. Night pushed Blaze away and slammed the laptop shut. He sat in his chair for a moment.

Swiveling back and forth slowly, trying to tame that savage part of him again. His eyes kept blinking from dark brown to amber.

"She probably came here to escape her reality," Blaze said. Night didn't answer his friend. He closed his eyes and focused on the spark of life inside of him that represented Trinity. It didn't feel the way it did the night before. Something had changed. More so, something was wrong with his little mate.

"I'll be back," Night said, pushing out of his chair. He grabbed his motorcycle keys.

"You're just gonna roll up into human town like it's cool?" Blaze asked.

"It's not illegal. Besides, something's wrong with her. I can feel it. And if she thinks she'd gonna marry that fucker, she's got another thing coming," Night declared.

"She belongs to me."

Night left his club after that, not needing to utter another word. He didn't care if he had to go to the human town in broad daylight. After just one taste of her body there was no going back for him. And he wasn't going to wait and watch as she got with some other man. He also didn't care if she didn't understand the vampire world yet. He was going to make her understand.

Feeling their small connection inside of him, Night used that as his GPS, allowing it to lead him to Trinity. When he spotted the mustang driving down the street, he knew he'd found his girl, and he stopped her immediately.

"Night, what are you doing here?" she asked, jumping out of her car.

"I could have run you over, that's the first thing!" she snapped.

"I'm over a 2 century old vampire, do you really think you would have been able to knock me down?" he asked her evenly. Trinity crossed her arms.

"Okay fine. And speaking of you being a vampire. How are

you here right now? In sunlight? In human town?" Night's brows dipped down.

"Do you really think I can have this deep of a sexy melanin and be unable to stand in the sun?" Night asked her.

"Those vampires afraid of the sun are of the Anglo-Saxon variety, and I'm far from that. Understand me?" he asked.

"Yes," Trinity swallowed. She looked him up and down. Sexy melanin sounded just about right. Her skin began to heat at his nearness.

"We need to have a conversation," he said.

"Oh—okay, alright. But let's go somewhere. People around here are nosey," Trinity said, knowing that at least one person was peeking out of the blinds watching her in the middle of the street with a sexy chocolate skinned vampire.

"Follow me to Emma's house. She's at work but I have a spare key to her place. We can talk there. She wouldn't mind," Trinity told him.

"I'm not following you anywhere. You're going to park that car somewhere and get on the back of my bike and we'll ride to Emma's together," he stated.

"But—but I can't just-" Night came forward, his hands behind his back. He leaned into her, barely brushing his lips against hers.

"It's not up for negotiation," he whispered. Trinity blinked rapidly, feeling as if she was going to fall into a puddle of arousal.

"My parents' house is just down the street. I'll park the car there and just walk back here to you," Trinity replied, swallowing the lump in her throat. Night looked at her for a little while. After staring at her, he moved towards the car. He kneeled down and grabbed under the front bumper, then stood, bringing the car upwards easily. Trinity's mouth fell open as she watched him pull the car effortlessly out of the street and against the curb. Once he set it down, he did the same to the back of the car, making sure it was parked straight.

"Supernatural strength," Trinity gasped.

"Get on," he said, pointing to his bike. Trinity was nervous but she moved like she had sense and went to his bike. He helped her climb onto the bike before climbing on in front of her. He pushed his helmet onto her head and revved up the bike. Trinity was in heaven as she rode on his beautiful motorcycle with her arms wrapped around his lean waist. When she closed her eyes she could envision herself on her own bike that she always dreamed of having, but being on Night's bike was just as good.

Through the rumble of the bike, and the helmet covering her mouth, she shouted the directions to Emma's home, directly into Night's ear. He didn't seem to have any problem hearing her. When they pulled up to Emma's home, be parked his bike in the back, kicking the stand out. He helped her down from the bike and pulled the helmet from her head.

"Are you okay darling?" he asked her.

"I'm—I'm fine," she stumbled. He nodded in approval before walking towards Emma's back porch and leaning against the wooden support beam on the porch.

"To what do I owe the pleasure now?" Trinity asked him.

"You are upset. How come?" he asked her. Trinity shifted nervously on her feet.

"Family problems. And you are angry and jealous. How come?" she countered, knowing exactly what he was feeling.

"Because you're engaged to some human named Trent. I found it on the internet," he replied, not holding back. Then again, Night wasn't a man who sugarcoated feelings.

"You were looking me up huh," Trinity said.

"What is this engagement all about? Do you love him? And if you do, why the hell were you allowing me to suck the life from your sweet little pussy before stamping the presence of my dick inside of you?"

"Don't talk like that!" Trinity urged. She didn't scold him because of embarrassment. She scolded him because her insides were beginning to flutter at his words. Never had a man aroused her by just his words or even his presence. Damn.

"It is the truth Trinity," he stated. She pouted at him, missing it when he called her 'darling.

"And what is that face for?" he asked her.

"I got used to you calling me darling," she shrugged, trying to act like it didn't bother her. She was such a sap. Night smiled warmly at her.

"I will keep that in mind darling," he responded. Instantly, her heart warmed.

"Tell me about this engagement. Do you love him?" he asked.

"No I don't love him Night. Besides, I'm not that kind of woman. If I'm committed to a man then I wouldn't cheat on him."

"What do you mean cheat? I don't understand it in that context," Night said. Trinity realized his age was truly showing. He'd grown up in a time where that word wasn't used in the way Trinity was using it now.

"I mean it in the sense of betraying. If I belonged to you Night, I wouldn't betray you and give my body to another man. I let you have my body because I don't want Trent."

"Then why are you marrying him?" Night asked.

"Because my family is forcing me to. Apparently if his family and my family combined forces it'll be like some huge power trip and they'd be the most superior family in this town. My mother and father signed a legal contract. If I don't marry Trent, then they're liable to get sued for everything they own. Think of it like the contracts in your club," Trinity explained.

"That's nonsense. You mean to tell me that out of all the

stupid laws you humans have, there's not one that says you can't be forced into marriage?" Night asked.

"At this point it's more like assets situation. Legally when it comes to assets, the law don't even care. In this town, my parents already own everything. Even the cops. There seems to be nothing I can do about it but to marry Trent. Or else they'll just get sued and lose their money and everything they've worked for. Part of me doesn't want to do that to my family but then again, I don't want to marry Trent. He doesn't even know how to satisfy me sexually. And he's an asshole." Night's eyes narrowed.

"You're not to let him touch you again. Ever," he ordered. Trinity found herself nodding. That was an order she could take.

"Either your parents get their heads out of their asses and fix this mess, or they're just going to end up poor," Night shrugged.

"Why do you say that?" Trinity asked.

"Because you're not marrying that asshole," he replied.

"And why is that?" she asked. Night leaned from the porch and walked up to her, invading her space again.

"Because I want you Trinity. And I'm not letting another man have you. It's as simple as that."

"You didn't even stop to think about what I want," Trinity declared. Night chuckled.

"I can feel your desires darling. I know you want me just as bad as I want you. Let's not pretend."

"Alright fine. I do want you. But what is this? Some fuck buddies' type of deal?" When his brows furrowed, she realized he didn't understand her.

"Fuck buddies are two people who just have carefree sex and like each other but they're not ready for a commitment or a relationship," Trinity explained.

"Maybe you misunderstand me darling. But I said I wanted

you. Not that I wanted to be your fuck bud, or whatever it is
you said. Vampires don't make such proclamations for someone
they just enjoy having sex with. Maybe humans have a
different understanding of what wanting someone means," he
said. Trinity began to understand that Night wasn't talking
about a simple hook up here and there. He was talking about
wanting her completely. Oddly enough, she wasn't afraid of it.

"What about Trent?" Trinity asked.

"As long as he keeps his hands off you, I'll let him live,"
Night shrugged.

"You'd kill him?!" Trinity gasped.

"I'm a vampire darling. We're always on the verge of being
savages. And if he touches what's mine, I promise I'll be every
bit of the monster humans fear." Trinity should have been
running from this man. She should have felt a spark of fear at
his threat, but the threat wasn't to her life and it was in her
honor. For some reason, it only made her want to get closer
to him.

"Night," she whispered.

"Yes darling?"

"I've wanted to be in your arms all morning," she admitted.
She pressed against him and wrapped her arms around his
neck. He pulled her close and dug his nose into her neck,
inhaling deeply.

"This morning, in the shower, I was touching myself and
wishing it were your hands," she whispered in his ear. He
cupped her bottom, and kneaded her flesh.

"Let us go inside," he said, his words laced with seduction.
Trinity pulled her ring of keys from her pocket where she kept
the spare key Emma had given to her. Night let her go slightly,
allowing her to walk to the backdoor and open it up. She waited
for Night to enter first but he pushed her inside first then came
in behind her and shut the door. Trinity quickly pulled her
phone from her pocket.

Em, Night came to see me and I had to get him out of sight so I brought him to your place. Even though Trinity had a spare key, she always let Emma know when she was at her place if Emma was still at work.

No worries Trin! And use the damn bed in the guest room. Don't fuck on my counters or my sofa! Trinity tucked her phone away with a smile on her face as she turned towards Night. He was looking around Emma's house.

"She has good taste," Night commented, liking the way Emma decorated. It smelled homey.

"She has the better taste of the two of us," Trinity said.

"Do you want something to drink?" Trinity offered motioning to the kitchen from where they stood in the living room.

"Your pussy juice. And then your blood." he replied, looking at her with a flash of amber colored eyes. Trinity swallowed.

"Well if you want me, you've gotta catch me," Trinity grinned. She began backing away to the hall where she could dart towards the guest bedroom. She looked at Night who hadn't moved an inch and thought she had the upper hand. She darted into the hall, attempting to run so he could catch her. She only ran a few feet when she ran into Night's strong chest. *Oomph!* She nearly fell back but Night caught her and threw her over his shoulder.

"Wait! How'd you get in front of me?!" Trinity screeched.

"I'm a vampire darling," was his reply. He kicked down the door to the guest bedroom and entered. He shimmied her body down his chest, keeping his arm around her waist. He yanked at her shorts with one hand while the other continued to hold her up.

"Are you saying you teleported?" she asked.

"I'm saying I can anticipate certain things and move faster than the human eye can track," he breathed. When he yanked her shorts down and off her legs, he threw the material on the ground.

"You've got no chair this time," she teased him. Night winked as he opened her thighs with his arms, placing both of them under her thighs. He hoisted her up until her thighs rested over his shoulders, putting her pussy lips directly in front of his mouth.

"I don't need a chair when my darling can just ride my face," he said, his breath tickling the moistness of her insides. Trinity clutched the top of his head, squeezing his locks as his tongue glided into her folds easily. He sucked her pussy lips into his mouth and began feasting like he was eating his Sunday dinner. Trinity grinded her hips against his mouth, moans escaping her throat. His lips tugged at her clit, sucking and slurping until her legs were trembling on top of his shoulders.

"I'm coming," Trinity gasped out, trying her best to hold herself up. Night's hands clutched at her back, keeping her steady as his tongue dug deeper into her. Her knees clamped against the side of his head as she jerked with her orgasm. One of his hands left her back and Trinity heard his belt buckle clack before the sound of his zipper opening. Her stomach tightened in anticipation once she heard that, eager to feel his length inside of her again. Night pulled at her lips, sucking up the last of her leaking juices before popping her clit from his mouth. His hands went to her hips and pulled her away from his face. Her legs dangled over his forearms as he held her up, guiding her down to his strained erection. Trinity wrapped her arms around his neck, kissing his lips lightly as their bodies connected. They groaned in unison as his length speared through her. Trinity's muscles tightened and then relaxed to accept his long and thick length.

"So tight," he grumbled as he began to move his hips, effectively stroking her. Trinity already felt her toes curling in the air as his length poked at her stomach. The floor next to them began to vibrate. Trinity glanced at the ground to see her phone screen lighting up. It had fell from the pocket of her shorts through the rough undressing by Night. She saw Trent's name across the screen.

"Trent's calling me," she groaned. Night clutched at her ass, using his supernatural strength to easily bounce Trinity up and down on his length.

"You say that man's name while I'm inside of you?" Night grunted. He brought her down hard on his length. Trinity's eyes widened as a sharp moan left her mouth.

"I'm sorry," she moaned, clutched the sides of his face, kissing him wildly as he pumped harder into her. Even with him moving her up and down, Trinity clenched her muscles and grinded against him.

"That feels so good darling," he groaned, tossing his head back. Trinity's toes curled even further when his stroke landed in the tight web of her g-spot. She clutched onto Night, feeling an orgasm about to implode her body.

"That's it darling. Come for me," he growled. He bounced her hips harder, forcing her to ride his dick whether she wanted to slow down or not. Trinity screeched, nearly losing her damn voice as she came hard, nearly shaking all the way out of his arms. With long strides, Night reached the bed in under a second and tossed her down. He grabbed her by the hips and quickly turned her over, pressing her face down into the mattress. He hiked her ass in the air and entered her deeply, continuing to stroke her g-spot like he owned it. Perhaps he truly did. Trinity's orgasm elongated, the sensation of the new position rocking her to the core. Her ass was clapping against Night's stomach as he drilled her, deepening each stroke. If anyone was walking by Emma's house, Trinity was pretty sure they could hear her screaming out holy hell under Night's superior stroke.

Juices were gushing out of her, her clit was quivering, and she was on the verge of passing out from so much pleasure. She felt his length begin to engorge before he slammed into her, and spilled his hot seed deep into her guts. If she wasn't human, she would fear he'd gotten her pregnant from the hefty amount of his release her pussy gulped down. *What if I wasn't human?* The thought crossed her mind swiftly, but it never left her conscience. Night leaned forward and Trinity felt his sharp teeth piercing through her shoulder. She gave into the bite, crying out in ecstasy as her walls tightened around his softening penis, achieving another orgasm just from his bite alone.

Her phone had continued to vibrate on the ground, but Trinity didn't care anymore. She couldn't care. Not after thunderous orgasms and a mind blowing bite.

"Do you feel better?" Night asked her.

"Much," she sighed, rolling over as he pulled himself from her.

"Are you sure I can't get pregnant?" Trinity asked.

"I am sure darling. It is impossible for you to carry my seed unless you are vampire or another form of supernatural being. Which I assure you, you are not," he replied.

"Oh," Trinity moped.

"Don't sound so let down," Night smiled at her. Trinity had always balked at the idea of children, running from the thought of having a round belly by a man she knew she wouldn't ever care about because her parents were running her damn life. Being with Night however was her choice, the best one she'd had in years and children to her now wasn't so daunting.

"Do you want to carry my seed?" Night asked her, as he went to her phone and picked it up from the ground. The way he posed the question sounded so easy but it hindsight it was a loaded question. Instinctively, she wanted to just say 'yes'. But then that human part of her that tried to find reason told her it was impossible for her to want something so committal to a man she hardly knew. But there was just a feeling inside of her, beating just as hard as her heart did. It was Night.

"What if I did?" Trinity whispered. Night glanced at her.

"You are a smart woman Trinity. You know what needs to be done in order for that to be possible," he replied.

"I know," she said casually. Night's thick brows rose, making Trinity melt at his sexy expression. What a man he was. He looked down at her phone in his hand and began scrolling. Trinity didn't care that he was scrolling through it, looking at the messages Trent had sent her.

"This is the way he talks to you?" Night asked, seeing how rude and crass Trent was through his texting.

"All the time," Trinity breathed. She shrugged it off as if it was okay. The savage part of Night that made his eyes start to burn orange wanting to rip this human to pieces for even daring to speak to Trinity in this matter. She belonged to Night and shouldn't be subjected to this kind of life.

"I will figure it out Night," Trinity said, sitting up. She felt the quiet storm brewing inside of him and knew that he wanted blood, and not to drink. She felt his anger and realized that Night could be as dangerous as humans feared vampires to be.

"Violence isn't going to help us. Being smart will. And I'll find a way. I know I will," Trinity vowed.

"Fine," he grunted.

"Let me go clean up. I have to get back home and see what the hell he wants from me," Trinity said, standing.

Night was quiet as he entered the bathroom with her, helping her to clean up and redress. He stayed quiet as he drove her back out to where they'd left the mustang on his bike. Even though he was quiet, they were still sharing moments through their connection from having each other's touch. As Trinity slid off his bike and gave him back his helmet, he leaned forward and pressed a kiss to her mouth. Trinity didn't care that they were out in broad daylight for everyone to see. This was her life, not anyone else's and she was going to kiss this sexy vampire who made her want to throw her life away and start a new one with him.

As Night rode off, Trinity couldn't help but stare after him. Could she throw her old life away? Could she start a new one with him? In his world?

Chapter Thirteen

Night was very unsettled even though he had the feel of his mate lingering on his body, her scent clutching at his skin. Despite her forced obligations, Trinity was perfectly fine, but Night didn't like the feeling he had in his gut when he thought about her living in another man's home, eating his food, having him linger around her, sniffing around like some dog. She was supposed to live with Night. He was the one who was supposed to feed her, supposed to take care of her, supposed to protect her. Not some asshole who wanted a contract signed to capture Trinity's hand. That wasn't love. That was some sick arrangement for selfish benefits.

When he returned to the club, Night attempted to get some work done, but Trinity was rampant in his mind. His gut was churning and burning with the urges to complete a mating bond with her. He needed to see her, needed to touch her or else he was just going to drive himself crazy.

"I don't understand. You could have easily brought her back here and forbid her to leave," Blaze shrugged. Night turned sharply and looked at his friend.

"In the time that you've met Trinity, do you honestly think I could drag her anywhere and forbid her to do anything?"

Night asked. If there was one thing he knew about Trinity, she wasn't easily shoved around. The only reason she was subjecting herself to the contract her parents put out on her was because of a good conscience. She didn't want them to lose their money or their work.

"She's a little firecracker, isn't she?" Blaze laughed.

"I wonder what she's doing?" Night pondered, looking out of the large window in his second-floor office.

"Go and see her again," Blaze suggested.

"It's only been 2 hours since I saw her last. She'll think I'm some kind of stalker," Night chuckled.

"You don't necessarily have to go as yourself," Blaze said. Night looked at Blaze again, a wicked grin spilling across his face.

"Can you take care of things around here?" Night asked.

"You know I got it." Blaze said.

"Now go. You smell of lust and sex and it's irritating," Blaze teased. Night pulled open the large glass windows and climbed up onto the sill. Blaze watched as Night stood on the window still, flexing his back muscles. After breathing in the sticky air of Louisiana, Night tilted forward and let himself fall from the window. Air whipped all around him and in his ears as he fell, gravity pulling him down to the ground. Before he could hit the ground and splatter into scrambled guts, Night spread his arms out and closed his eyes. His body transformed swiftly, jet black feathers spouted from his skin as his body vibrated and snapped into the figure of a large black raven. He swooped into the sky, spreading his magnificent wings just before he hit the ground. The vampires in town who saw his flight whooped and cheered, knowing who was truly inside of the large bird, flying above them. His heart was pattering with wild excitement at the thought of being close to Trinity again. His Trinity.

TRINITY SAT in the mustang for quite some time, fighting the jitters and bubbles of happiness threatening to shoot out of her body. She could still feel Night's lips against hers and if she closed her eyes, she could imagine the kisses all over again. There were no physical marks on her body but she felt as if Night's presence was stamped all over her. That anyone could look at her and know that Night had touched her, and caressed her, and made incredible love to her body. She looked down at her stomach.

"It can't happen," she groaned, throwing her head back against the headrest and sighed loudly. She closed her eyes to calm her racing heart. She smiled as an image of Night lingered through her mind. He was smiling at her in that way that made her heart stop before it began fluttering intensely. What she thought was just an image of her Night slowly changed as if she was dreaming. She saw herself sitting in a large bed, leaning against Night. He was smiling down at her as he carefully kissed her cheek and then her neck, his large hand slowly caressing her round and very pregnant stomach.

Trinity jumped up, tearing her eyes open. Her heart was racing as she looked all round her.

"What the fuck?" She clutched at her chest, attempting to calm herself down.

"I must have fallen asleep," she sighed, trying to find an explanation as to why she was seeing herself pregnant with Night. She grasped at her phone and looked at the screen. Either she was losing her mind or she'd only fallen asleep for five minutes. She was probably thinking so hard about being pregnant by Night, she was seeing things. That was perfectly reasonable. She swiped on the screen of her phone unlocking it. The last thing she was looking at on her phone popped up on her screen.

How to become a vampire. She read the caption in Google that she'd typed in the search engine. She chuckled at herself and closed the tab before tossing her phone in the passenger seat.

"You're just sprung as fuck," she laughed at herself.

"Of course, you can't be a damn vampire," she shook her head. She started up the Mustang and headed back to the part of her life that brought her dread.

Trinity thought that Trent would be storming at her the moment she entered the house, but when she tip toed through the back door, it was completely quiet. Vickie was in the kitchen stirring away viciously at cake batter.

"Well then, come here missy!" she snapped. Trinity opened her mouth to make an excuse but Vickie rushed over and grabbed her by the elbow.

"Try this, now! Tell me what you think," Vickie said, shoving a dish of peach cobbler in front of Trinity. Vickie sliced her a piece and nearly shoved it down Trinity's throat. Trinity didn't dare object as she opened her mouth and let Vickie feed her.

"Hmmm, so good!" Trinity said, the sweet and sticky peaches lighting up her taste buds.

"Good. I can serve this at the dinner party Trent will be hosting."

"Dinner party?" Trinity asked. "When is it?"

"That's your fiancé. Don't he tell you nothing?" Vickie asked.

"I'm not exactly fond of the man, you see. I'm marrying him because a piece of paper says I have to," Trinity admitted. Vickie nodded her head.

"Listen to me girl. My mother told me to marry this man. His name was Charles. All the ladies wanted him; all the men wanted to be him. He was a sweet, good looking man. But he couldn't keep it in his pants, see. He got with any girl that so much bat her lashes at him. I was not going to be with a man like that. Despite his money, and my parents pleading that they needed the arrangement to secure our family name, I outright refused. I didn't care about my future or my family or anything. Just my pride."

"What happened?" Trinity asked.

"I'm here, working as a maid and servant, living in a small room in one of the biggest houses in Louisiana, single with no children. What do you think happened? I should have listened to my mother child, and maybe you should listen to yours. Despite what you think of Trent, he will take care of family and home and you won't end up like me." She nodded firmly at Trinity. Trinity slowly stood.

"Where is Charles now? Do you know?" Trinity asked.

"Last I heard, he married some gal who ended up breaking his poor heart. But he's so rich, it doesn't even matter." Trinity looked at the woman and saw in her the sadness that Trinity often felt. She quickly pulled her phone from her pocket and did another Google search. It wasn't hard to find information on a man named Charles in Louisiana who was rich.

"Is this him?" Trinity asked turning her phone over.

"Oh my, yes it is," Vickie gasped.

"You're right, it says he is divorced. And there's a phone number. Maybe you should call him."

"Don't be silly child," Vickie waved her off.

"I don't see why not. You're clearly unhappy."

"My time has passed. I should have listened and I didn't. These are the repercussions of my actions. It is life child."

"What you did Vickie, was follow your heart. Who's to say you wouldn't have ended up far worse married to a man that betrayed your vows? Life has it's lessons Vickie and it's not about what your mom wanted or that you should have listened. It's about following your heart. Sometimes things align the way it's supposed to. Maybe poor Charles needed a heartbreak to finally realize that you can't buy love. He'll be more than happy to have someone genuine in his life. Your life isn't over Vickie, there's no deadline on starting over. Not marrying a man because of his lack of faithfulness didn't land you as a maid. Maybe people have told you that, but they're wrong. Don't let people have power over you in that way." Trinity smiled at the woman before scribbling down Charles' number on a piece of mail sitting on the table. She shoved it towards Vickie then left the kitchen.

In that entire speech, Trinity just wanted to slap herself. She was preaching about starting over and not letting people control you, but here she was still in Trent's house, looking for him instead of in the arms of Night. Oh, his warm protective arms. Trinity shivered and hugged herself. Even thinking about his arms made her sore with longing. She had to get out of this shit. She wanted Night. Even if it was just the goodness of the dick talking, she didn't care. It was her life and it was supposed to be about what she wanted, not what would benefit everyone else.

"I'm back!" Trinity called. She went up the large grand staircase towards the master bedroom. She walked down the hall towards the bedroom.

"Trent! Trent!" The shrilling moans gave Trinity pause. She stopped completely and listened. Trent was grunting.

"You like it don't you," his voice rumbled. Trinity's mouth fell open.

"I love it! I love it!"

"Now you know you lying! Short stroke Trent cannot fuck," Trinity said, rolling her eyes. She tiptoed towards the room. The door was halfway open, enough for Trinity to peak her head inside. They were on the bed, missionary style. Her panties hanging off one of her ankles above her heels, while his pants were down around his thighs. Clearly, they hadn't had time to fully undress. Trent's ass was squeezed together as he thrusted inside of her with force, grunting like a madman. Her moans were shrill as she clutched him, gripping at his shirt.

When he dipped down to kiss her neck and she brought her head forward, Trinity saw exactly who it was. She shook her head and backed away from the door.

"Please take him and get him out of my life," Trinity whispered, praying that catching another woman fucking her "fiancé" would be Trinity's way out of this whole mess.

She rushed away from the bedroom and down the stairs, nearly falling flat on her face as she tripped down the stairs in her haste to leave. Instead of leaving through the backdoor, she went straight out the front door, not caring what servant saw her leaving or if Trent heard the massive doors opening. She ran out into the courtyard, stopping in the center of the circular driveway. Looking around at the large gates surrounding the property, she felt even more trapped. Running wasn't ever going to fix this. How could she truly get rid of this man? This contract? This stupid life she was being forced into? She walked around towards the back of the house, going to the garden, needing time to just think.

The bush next to her rustled, putting Trinity on high alert. A large raven, seemingly coming out of thin air flew directly at her, and then right over her head. Trinity squealed and covered her head with her arms just in case the bird was going to attack. Instead, it just flew over her and perched on the roof of the house.

"Damn bird!" Trinity complained, throwing her fist up at it as if threatening the animal. The bird looked right at her and tilted his head in the way that pigeons did. Trinity shook her head and continued to walk towards the garden. She looked back at the bird who was still watching her.

"Betta stay over there!" she yelled at it, not wanting to have to fight for her life against a bird that was bigger than her whole face.

In the solace of the garden, she sat on the swing chair, swinging lightly as she looked out at the rainbow of growth.

There were two young women tending to the garden. Even though it was their jobs, their faces showed content as if this was their life's work. In a way, tending a garden was something to be proud of. Being in charge of life had immense responsibility. The younger of the two women came over to Trinity, handing her a yellow tulip.

"It'll look good in your hair," she said, smiling at Trinity's curls. Agreeing with her, Trinity put the flower behind her ear so it blended with her curls. The girl walked away then, leaving Trinity to her thoughts. The sound of soft screeching caught her ear. Looking to her left, she saw the large bird sitting on the fence just outside the garden. Trinity jumped and clutched her heart, the bird seemingly larger now that it was closer. It slowly lifted off then flew lazily towards Trinity. It landed on the fountain next to the swing chair and just stayed there. Trinity was afraid it would jump on her until she saw the raven fluff its feathers out and dipped one of its wings into the water of the fountain then let the water from its wing drip onto its head as if trying to cool itself off. Trinity smiled.

"You're big but kind of cute," she spoke. The bird looked at her and cooed.

"Sorry I threatened you earlier. You're just an innocent animal and these people in my life are driving me up a fucking wall," Trinity sighed. The bird cocked its head again, as if it could understand Trinity.

"See, there's this sexy ass vampire right. And then there's Trent. But why on earth would I choose Trent over my sexy vamp? There's no effin' comparison." The raven chucked and spread its wings, shaking them out before settling again.

"I thought I heard you out here," Vickie said, coming out of the back door with a tray carrying a glass off sweet tea and a plate of cookies.

"Thanks Vickie," Trinity smiled as Vickie placed the drink and cookies on the lawn table near the swing chair. She left immediately, not engaging in anymore conversation with Trinity. Shrugging, Trinity took a few sips of the sweet tea and ate a cookie. She held out one of the cookies for the raven.

"Want some crumbs?" she asked it. The bird shook it's head. Trinity froze and just stared at it.

"Umm, alright," she said, trying not to run away from the bird who seemed completely harmless but apparently just shook it's head to a question she asked.

Trinity stayed in the swing, the heat of the day not bothering her with the shade and the cool drink in her hand. Her mind was crazed with thoughts about Trent and her family, and Trinity found herself talking to the large bird to get her feelings out. Still, she didn't know what she was going to do.

The backdoor slammed open, disrupting Trinity's sanctuary. She jumped at the sound of the door hitting the brick wall and looked at Trent who came out of the house. His mouth was stretched to a thin line, his brows furrowed in his obvious anger.

"Vickie told me you were out here. Where in the fuck have you been? I've been calling, and texting and I get not one response from you!" he snapped.

"Really? I don't have any missed calls or texts. I've been here," Trinity shrugged, looking up at him and squinting her eyes from the sun.

"Do you think that this is some kind of joke?" Trent asked her.

"You tell me Trent," she replied lazily, putting her glass to her lips and taking another sip.

"I'm hosting a dinner party tonight. Go find something to wear and put it on so I can see how it looks on you. Then I want your damn hair straightened," Trent ordered. The raven sitting at the fountain crowed and flapped its wings angrily towards Trent.

"What the hell?! Get outta here!" Trent picked up a rolled-up newspaper and threw it at the raven, hitting it.

"Hey! Cut that out!" Trinity said, standing. Trent ignored her and continued to shoo the bird away, waving his arms and lunging at it. The bird squawked and flew off.

"You're such an ass. It was an innocent animal!" Trinity exclaimed.

"That's enough out of you! You're gonna go inside and do what I said. You're going to respect me and act as my fiancée when our guests arrive and you're gonna do what I tell you. Is that understood?"

"She must have not been a good fuck," Trinity said, standing casually.

"Excuse me?" he snapped.

"Not half an hour ago you were pounding some woman's pussy out talking about 'do you love it', now you're out here in my face grumpy as shit. I would have thought that a good fucking would have made you less of an asshole. Clearly not." Trent just glared at her, his mouth opening and closing as he tried to find something to say to her.

"Trinity, I-"

"I saw you Trent. I saw your tight little ass squeezing as you fucked her half clothed on your bed. You don't have to lie about it," she shrugged.

"It meant nothing. I was just angry with you, and I—I had a few drinks and-"

"I just struggle with the fact that you were fucking another woman not too long ago and now you're in my face demanding I act like your fiancée. Don't get me wrong, I don't care who you fuck Trent. But if you want to fuck other women then force those other women to be your fiancée. Not me."

"Because it is you I want and your family is the one that signed the contract for me to have you," he stated.

"Bullshit," Trinity muttered.

"Despite whatever you saw Trinity, no one would ever believe that I actually did that. They'd know that I'm a man of commitment. So, don't even think about getting out of your contract. You have no proof and besides, you wouldn't want to look like you're making up stories, now would you? People might think you're out of your mind."

"You wouldn't dare start that kind of rumor!" Trinity snapped at him.

"Try me, Trinity. Please do."

"I don't have to take this shit," she stated, turning to leave.

"Don't you dare walk away from me, get your ass in this house!" Trent snatched her elbow, yanking her towards him.

"Get your fucking hand off me!" Trinity turned around and threw her sweet tea in his face. *Squawk!* The large black raven swooped down over Trinity's head, its wings flapping violently as it attacked Trent. With its talons and beak, the raven scraped at Trent's face and drilled at his head. Trent finally let Trinity go, sending her falling to the ground. She fell on her behind, scooting away quickly as she watched the bird flapping its wings and digging its talons into Trent's head and neck.

"You fucking bird! Get the fuck off me!" Trent fought valiantly against the animal, but Trinity wasn't sticking around to see the outcome. The bird had chosen the perfect time to exact it's revenge against Trent and Trinity was using it to make her getaway. She had to go the long way around to get back into the house and snatch up the mustang keys again. She heard Trent shouting and cursing but she didn't stop or turn back for a second.

Knowing it would probably result in nothing, but still willing to try; Trinity drove back to her parents' home. When she went inside, she found her parents and her sister in the master bedroom. Her mother was showing her father an array of dresses.

"This one. I like this one. You'll look lovely in it," James said, approving his wife's dress.

"Trinity, you should be back home preparing for the dinner party tonight," Rose scolded, seeing Trinity burst into the room.

"And honey, you look a hot mess. Please, you can't walk around town like this." In her t-shirt and shorts and no makeup, she knew it wasn't the approved way for her to look.

"There has to be some clause or some way for me to get out of this contract," Trinity got straight to the point. Her parents and her sister laughed at her.

"Honey, we try to tell you. There's just no way. Now go on back home and get ready for the dinner party. We're excited for the event tonight," Rose smiled.

"Stop saying that! That place is not my home. Hell, I have no home. Not here or there!"

"I'm getting tired of this talk," James stated. He gave Trinity a look of disgust before he was storming out of the room. Trinity looked at her mother.

"You need to do something about this," Trinity demanded.

"And what the hell do you want me to do? The contract is said and done!" Rose exclaimed.

"If you can live your best life, then guess what? I'm gonna do whatever the hell I want to."

"You're so fucking selfish Trinity!" Tracee snapped at her. Trinity looked at her sister.

"Okay so then how about this, you marry Trent then," Trinity snapped back.

"Don't be ridiculous! Trent chose you!" Rose stated.

"We have to make sacrifices for family Trinity. This is your sacrifice! Suck it up!" Trinity shook her head and forced her tears to remain at bay.

"I would sacrifice anything for a family who gave a fuck about how I felt. But the both of you are liars and hypocrites!"

"Excuse me?!" Rose exclaimed clutching her chest.

"Oh don't play that fucking prissy act. Remember what the hell I caught you doing and where I caught you doing it.

Oh, and your daughter over here? I saw you," Trinity sneered.

"Saw me, what?!" Tracee asked, her voice shaky.

"Fuck me harder Trent, oh, I love it, I love it!" Trinity mocked the way her sister sounded.

"She fucked Trent, and I caught her doing it. I'm the one written on the contract and I'm the one being forced to marry Trent, but Tracee was the one just fucking him and then coming here acting like she's some little saint. Why am I being forced to marry the bastard when he clearly wants to fuck her and Tracee clearly wants to get fucked?" Rose gasped and looked at Tracee.

"How could you do that to your sister?" Rose asked. Tracee held her head down, unable to speak.

"That's not even the point mother! If she can fuck him, then she can marry him!" Trinity snapped. She looked at her mother and sister before she stormed out of the house, feeling as if she was going to explode. The sun was still out and Trinity felt as if she'd been through the damn ringer.

She rushed into the Mustang and drove off before anyone could run out and stop her. Running out of options of places to go, Trinity motored towards Emma's home. She didn't care if Emma was home or not, but she just needed a place that felt safe. A place where she knew her family wasn't going to follow her to. They could go to that dinner party and pretend everything was fine and dandy but Trinity couldn't. She couldn't fake it anymore.

She parked sloppily in Emma's driveway. When she shut the car off, she finally took a deep breath but, on the exhale, a small spattering of tears hit her cheeks.

"Don't cry over them," she scolded herself, trying to lock back in her tears.

"Don't let them have control." *Squawk!* Trinity jumped out of her skin as the large raven landed with a heavy plop against the hood of the mustang. Trinity screeched in her fright and clutched her chest.

"You goddamn bird! How are you even here?!" Trinity shouted. This wasn't a different raven. It was the same large raven that she'd spoken to in Trent's garden. How could it possibly have followed her? Trinity slid out of the car, careful not to rattle the bird that sat on the roof.

"You get on out of here now. I'm not in the mood," she spoke calmly. The bird jumped from the hood but before it landed on the ground, Trinity was blown back with a power surge. A black puff of smoke nearly stifled her. She coughed and fanned it away quickly. When she was finally able to open her eyes, it wasn't a large raven looking up at her. Night was hovering over her, his lips a mere inch away from hers. He brushed at the tears that stained her cheeks.

"Night? But—how?" Trinity gasped.

"You know the whole story about vampires changing into bats? It's true but evolution has allowed us to change into other winged creatures. I am sorry I did not protect you more from that horrible man," Night said.

"Oh Night." Trinity shuddered as she fell against his bare chest. He enclosed her in his arms, hugging her tightly while whispering sweet words in her ear.

"You're coming with me, right now," Night said, massaging her neck. Trinity looked up at him and sniffled.

"Why didn't you reveal yourself before?" she asked.

"Because I didn't want you to think I was stalking you or something. But to be apart from you Trinity is like having my heart snatched from my chest. I do not like it. Come back with me to the club. Look what these people have done to you." He brushed at another tear that escaped her eye. At this point, Trinity wasn't going to refuse. She wanted to be anywhere but here.

"You can drive," she said, nodding to the keys still inside

the Mustang. Night nodded. He walked her to the passenger side and helped her in the car. As he walked around, Trinity noticed he had pants on.

"How can you shapeshift and return back to normal with clothes on?" Trinity asked him. He adjusted the seat and mirrors before backing out of the driveway.

"It's my magic," Night replied.

"Wait?! You have magic?!" Trinity squealed.

"Not in the sense of a fairy or a witch. But I can will things to do what I want them to do. I can change into a raven and cast some spells. Fairly simple things," Night shrugged. Trinity was just staring at him, wondering how he was saying this was a simple thing.

"Do you have visions?" she asked.

"I can have visions of past events or premonitions but I cannot control those events." Night glanced at Trinity briefly to see she was deep in thought.

"Why do you ask darling?" he questioned.

"I had a vision. Either it was a vision or a premonition. But you were in it. I don't know if maybe your powers were just projecting on me or something."

"What was the vision about?"

"Just us," she shrugged. Night could tell in her voice that there was more to it, but he didn't force her into an explanation. Her visions were most likely result of their mate bond growing within them, linking them together and bonding them. It was like how she could tell what he was feeling, and he could do the same with her. Night reached over and took her hand, caressing her wrist as he felt her anxiety rise.

"Be easy my darling. You're with me now," he vowed. Through their thumping bond, Night felt her mind relax, her body ease and a small smile touch her face. That was satisfying enough for Night.

THE CLUB WAS A COMPLETELY DIFFERENT ATMOSPHERE when the sun was out. In fact, the entire vamp town was different with the sun beaming down, giving warm light to the atmosphere. As they drove through town, Trinity sat forward, looking through the window. From the lawns of homes, little vampire children were waving excitedly at Night as they drove by. The grown-ups were walking around leisurely, enjoying drinks and the sun and the company of their families. You wouldn't see anything like this where Trinity lived. All of her neighbors hid behind their large gates and luxurious lawns and gardens, but were always peeking out of their windows at the first sign of a simple disturbance.

"Everyone looks so happy," Trinity commented. She sat back and sighed, wondering when her happiness was going to begin to trickle in.

"Ask me for anything Trinity, and I will give it to you," Night spoke softly, next to her.

"Anything?" Trinity questioned.

"Anything," Night repeated. She heard the conviction of his voice and knew that he wouldn't make such a pledge without meaning it. Vampires didn't need to make useless promises and sell false dreams.

Night pulled around to the back of the club and parked the Mustang next to his motorcycle. Trinity got out of the car and admired the bike, wanting to ride it again.

"You can always take it for a spin darling," he offered.

"Really?!" Trinity gasped.

"Yes." He took her hand, pulling her close to his body before wrapping his arm around her waist. He held her close and they walked around to the front of the club to enter. They passed a few vampires on their short trip around to the front of the club, and where Trinity thought they would turn their noses up at her, they instead were smiling at her, showing off their fangs with pride.

The atmosphere of the club was completely different than its nighttime counterpart just like the rest of vamp town. The place was brightly lit and full of vampires lounging, eating, enjoying music, and even playing cards. Children were running around having fun with each other and Trinity realized everyone in the club was part of a family. They were treating the club as the living room, and just enjoying the space without the intrusion of humans.

Trinity was nervous, being the only human in the club at this hour, but Night didn't loosen his hold around her waist. When the other vampires noticed him, they acknowledged his presence. Night took her around to each of the vampires who'd called for his attention. Before he said anything to them in regards to their concerns, he immediately introduced her.

"This is my special lady, Trinity," he said. Every vampire smiled at her but then they would inhale deeply and gasp as if she smelled funky. Trinity thought they would all call her out on being human but after their initial reactions of surprise, they would bow their heads and greet her kindly. Trinity was used to having men be sweet to her because of who her parents were and because they were only trying to butter her up, but she sensed a true genuineness in these reactions. Not only that, but even the women and the children had the same reactions. Trinity didn't understand it.

After Night listened and spoke with the vampires who needed his attention, he took her up to his office where they were alone.

"Why did they all do that? Smell me and then bow? What were they surprised at? That I'm a human?" Trinity asked.

"Because even if I am a human, I'm not here to just use you or take advantage. And I certainly don't want to be bowed down to because they think I'm some high-class human that's above them. What was that all about?" Night gazed at her and smiled.

"You are amazing Trinity. Truly. I admire you for the fact that you don't want to be a human that thinks they're better than everyone. Especially because your family is rich and owns half the town. But they were not bowing to you for that reason. Those vampires down there I consider my family. And no family of mine is bowing down to no human. We're far superior in strength and intelligence. Not to you of course darling, because you're one of a kind."

"Why were they bowing then?"

"Because I am their leader. I scent marked you and because they bow to me, they will bow to you."

"Scent marked me?" Trinity asked.

"Everyone has a scent that is specific to them. I took my scent and I wove it into yours the first time we fucked."

"Why?" Trinity asked with a smile.

"Because I knew I would want you and it was a possessive thing that I had to do for my own satisfaction. I have not marked a woman in this way for a long time. This is a monumental event," he said.

"If you can mark me then I want to mark you," Trinity declared.

"Don't worry darling, you already have. Your special scent carries around with me and all the vampires can smell it and now they can recognize who it belongs to because I have introduced you to them," Night replied. Trinity closed the distance between them and rose to her tippy toes. She kissed him softly. A blissful sigh left her mouth. How could one man's kiss turn her to mush?

"Something changes when I'm with you, Night. It doesn't make sense, and it defies reason but I just—you make me lust harder than I've ever had before," Trinity admitted.

"You turn me inside out just the same darling," he replied, holding the side of her neck, lifting her head for another kiss. Their tongues mingled slowly, sweet and yearning. More. Trinity needed more.

"Where is he?! I don't give a fuck!" *Slam!* The door to Night's office slammed against the wall as a crazed looking woman barged into the office. Night yanked Trinity behind him, in a protective stance. Her head rattled at the quickness of the movement.

"I tried to tell her she couldn't just come up here, but she wouldn't listen," Blaze informed Night.

"You damn right I didn't listen. You had my underage daughter in this club fucking one of your beasts! She's only 17! I'm getting the cops in here and I'm getting this club shut down with a lawsuit! Who was the monster that raped my daughter? Once I call in this crime that vampire is gonna get his damn head chopped off!" Night remained calm as the woman shouted at him.

"Your daughter came in here willingly. She also had sex willingly. We have video proof that shows that."

"Willingly or not you ignorant monster, at 17 years old, that's still rape. Who did it?! You give me the name of the culprit or so help me I'm getting this entire place closed the fuck down with lawsuits. Try me monster. Who do you think the courts will side with? Me? Or your blood sucking nasty ass?" Trinity poked her head out from behind Night, her mouth agape at the way the woman was talking to him. Trinity didn't recognize her, but by the way she was dressed she was one of those 'my shit don't stink' nose upturned type of woman.

"My name is Night. You will do well to call me that," Night said to her.

"Does it look like I give a damn what your name is, fucking Dracula. Who raped my daughter?!" she screamed.

"I had sex with your daughter," Night shrugged. Trinity turned sideways so quickly, looking at Night.

"You're going down. I'm going to sue you for everything you've got!"

"Are you aware that all participants of the club must sign a contract before indulging in any of the activities?" Night asked.

"What are you talking about?" she questioned.

"Your daughter signed a contract for sex. Once the contract is signed, she's granting permission for things to be done to her body. If you don't like that, well take that up with your child. I had sex with your daughter because she signed a contract that told me I could. Legally, me and my club are protected. If she lied about her age, that is not of my concern. Shall I get the paperwork for you to see? Would you like to bring that to the police and tell them that your daughter signed a contract to be fucked by a vampire even though she was underaged?" Night asked. The woman shifted uncomfortably.

"But—my little girl is pregnant. You're responsible for this and I don't care what paperwork you have. Since you can run this club you're gonna give me all the money I need to raise my grandchild that you put in my daughter!"

"Wow, don't you know? I'm a vampire. My semen don't work. If your daughter's pregnant, it surely isn't mine. Maybe it wasn't just a vampire your daughter wanted a fuck from," Night shrugged. The woman gasped.

"How dare you talk to me like that?! Oh! I got something for your ass!" She dug into her large purse and pulled out a small spray bottle. She began to spray the contents of the bottle onto Night.

"Go back to hell you devil!" she screeched. Night covered his face from the spray and Trinity immediately realized she was trying to hurt Night with holy water. Trinity stepped out from behind Night immediately.

"What the hell are you doing?!" Trinity rushed up to the woman and snatched the bottle away from her.

"Are you out of your fucking mind?" Trinity snapped.

"Tri—Trinity Kayne?" the woman blinked, shocked at who stood in front of her.

"Who the fuck do you think you are? This is this man's place of business! And what? Because your daughter is hot in the pants you come up in here on his property in his fucking face? This is a legitimate business but because he's a vampire you think you can come in here and say and do whatever the fuck you want without repercussion? You're trespassing and you just assaulted him. Those are crimes!"

"Assault?! Please!" she exclaimed. Trinity held out the bottle.

"This is holy water and because you believe it would do him harm you used it against him. That's fucking assault. So unless you want me to call the cops, I suggest you pack your shit up and get out."

"When did you become their damn advocate?!" she snapped.

"Last chance. Get out willingly. Or I'll put you out myself, and then you can try to slap a charge on me and see how well it does for you." Trinity glared at the woman, daring her to say something else. She grunted at Trinity and grabbed the spray bottle before rushing out of the office.

"And if you ever come back here you're gonna have to deal with me!" Trinity shouted after her. She slammed the office door and turned around quickly to Night.

"Are you okay?" she asked hastily, fearing the holy water had burned him. Night was glaring at her, his eyes full on amber.

"Blaze. Please leave," Night instructed. Without question, Blaze left the office and shut the door again.

"You'd take up for me? Without knowing how it would affect you in the end?" Night asked.

"Yes, I'd take up for you! I'd protect you from all these stuck-up ass humans! She had no right to come up in here and spray you with holy water. And I know it was that young vampire that had sex with that girl and you lied to protect him. It's only right that someone protect you too. They think they can come up here and talk to you like that in your place of business? A place you built from the ground up? Oh hell no! I'm claiming you, Night. So that means ain't nobody gonna talk to you any type of crazy without hearing my mouth. Trust and believe that!" Trinity stated. The intensity of emotion she felt for Night thumped through her body, making her feel like she had one giant pulse. The energy that belonged to him that was growing inside of her body seemed to grow larger and larger.

With bright burning eyes, Night grabbed her and smashed his mouth down on hers, kissing her intensely.

"I'm burning with desire for you," he growled.

"Take me, Night. Fuck, just take me. I'm yours," Trinity moaned. Night scooped her into his arms. The room spun, and she felt the sudden brush of air against her skin. Light zoomed over her vision, and when her eyes adjusted, she saw they were in Night's bedroom. All in a matter of seconds.

Night set her down and just glared at her. His eyes were

burning a hole through her but Trinity wasn't afraid. The sheer power radiating off his body made the air in the room hot and sticky, threatening to stifle her. Sweat beaded against her temples, as her breathing became labored. Her heart began to constrict, feeling as if it would combust for the outrageous need she felt when she looked at Night.

"Why do I feel like this?" she asked him hoarsely.

"Like if I don't have you, I'll lose my damn mind," she breathed, clutching at her curls.

"Maybe that's just the way it is," Night replied.

"Let me see all of you," Trinity begged of him. Night yanked his shirt from his body and his jeans came off just as swiftly. Trinity felt the decrease in control of her breathing functions again. His locks swayed over his shoulders from the motion of his undressing. The dark locks long against his body, falling over his toned stomach made Trinity's stomach quake. Her eyes lowered to his thick patch of pubic hair, before the length of his dick began to thicken and grow. Her breath hitched. It was hers. It belonged all to her. She didn't care if she wasn't supposed to make such a vow. She wanted this man more than she needed to breathe.

"That's not all of you," Trinity gulped. A smile teased the corner of his mouth. His fangs dipped from his gums, long, thick and sharp. Claws stretched from his nails, dangerously sharp. His eyes continued to glow but burned brighter. It matched the sun that was setting just out of the window, casting orange shadows across the room.

Trinity closed the distance between her and Night. She raised her hand and used the tip of her fingers to caress his tight stomach, easing his locks out of the way. She took him by the wrist and placed his clawed hand on her chest. He grasped the material of her shirt, and shredded it under his claws deliberately. She didn't flinch but her head fell back as a moan escaped her mouth from the erotic feeling of having her clothes shredded from her body. She stayed completely still as he repeated the same notion with her shorts, and then pulled the material completely off of her.

"You've never been afraid of me," Night said, cupping her perfect breasts in his large hands. He was incredibly careful, making sure not to nick her pretty skin with his claws.

"There's a part deep down inside of me that tells me that I should never be afraid of you," Trinity moaned, as he rolled her nipples. He pulled her body into his, his dick stabbing her in the stomach. With an arm wrapped around her waist, he clutched her bottom while pushing her breast into his mouth. He picked up her left leg, and hung it over the crook in his arm. She went up on her tip toes on her right foot, trying to match his height as he lifted her left leg high enough to open her up. His engorged tip, beading with tears of arousal brushed against her pussy lips that too were weeping. A shudder left his mouth that was still latched around her breast as he eased himself inside of her. His claws gripped her bottom tightly, nicking her slightly.

Trinity eyes rolled to the back of her head as he filled her up, stretching her almost beyond her capacity. He was so long, he was able to fuck her standing up, and thrust deep enough to touch the cavernous part of her that needed to be touched. It was as if Night knew her body more than she knew it. He knew the perfect way to tilt his hips, he knew that she liked her guts to be knocked on until she answered the door with an earth-shattering orgasm. She screamed out, riding his delish choco-latey goodness as her muscles tightened and ached. She clutched his shoulder and brought her head forward, biting into his shoulder as if she had her own pair of fangs that could pierce into his skin and take his blood within her body. Night grunted, the effect of her blunt teeth biting him, throwing him into a sudden orgasm. With her breast in his mouth, he bit down, easing his fangs into her pillows of softness. Trinity's body jerked as the bite struck her the same time he thumped against her g-spot. Her eruption came in a silent scream as the shock of it paralyzed her to everything. She lost all sense of time and light, everything went black as she came, the only crippling feeling she could sense was the plowing orgasm and the sucking of her blood. Then nothing.

Chapter Fifteen

CONSCIOUSNESS SLOWLY REGISTERED IN TRINITY'S BRAIN. Her eyes opened slowly, still heavy with sleep. The room was dark except for the moonlight drifting through the curtains. She slowly sat up and looked around. The bedroom was empty and so was the space in the bed next to her. *Where was he?* Even still being at the club, not waking up in his arms saddened her. She felt like a child who needed to wake and find someone next to them to feel safe. Only, this wasn't just about feeling safe. It was about feeling whole.

Trinity left the comfort of the satin sheets and tip toed around the bed. She peeked out of the bedroom door and found the hall dark and quiet. Standing there completely naked, she couldn't just venture to Night's office to find him. When she closed the door and turned around, she spotted the settee pushed up against the far wall. A short red slip was laid across the small couch along with a basket of shower gel, shampoo, and shea butters. The door in the corner was slightly ajar, revealing the tiled floor in the dark room. Trinity could guess it was the bathroom. She grabbed the basket and went to the bathroom, impressed with the luxury of the bathroom. She started the luxurious spray of water inside of the shower.

She spent 20 minutes under the spray of the water, turning the dial on the showerhead to change the way the water came out. The bathroom was completely steamed over when she finally cut the water off and wrapped herself in a fluffy towel. Back in the bedroom, a large tray was waiting for her on the bed. Curious, she went to the bed and picked up the cloche that covered a plate piled high with food.

Sorry you have woken without me next to you. There is much work to do within the club tonight. But fear not darling, I shall return to your loving arms soon. For now, enjoy this meal and continue to rest. I have told Emma where you are, no need to worry about anyone else. Night.

Trinity smiled at the handwritten note. She didn't even know where her phone was, but she was appreciative to that fact that Night made it a point to mention that she didn't have to worry about anyone who might be concerned with her whereabouts except for Emma. She didn't have to worry about her family or Trent. Knowing that fact, she could easily smile as she ate the meal brought up to her. Her long hot shower and a delicious meal that filled her stomach, Trinity crawled back into the bed after pulling on the red slip. Her idea was to just wait until Night returned to the bedroom, but her body had an entirely different idea, and she was back in a deep slumber with ease.

TRINITY DIDN'T HAVE to open her eyes to know that Night was with her. Her body had come alive with awareness. That scent he talked about before, Trinity felt it surrounding her, invading her senses.

"Oh Night," she moaned.

"I was hoping you wouldn't wake yet," he whispered. Trinity felt her legs lifting. She snapped her eyes open in time to see her legs latched to the headboard over her head. She looked out at Night who was kneeling in front of her open legs, licking his lips at the display of her pussy lips in front of him.

"I wanted to wake you with my tongue," he hummed, lowering his head to her opening. The tip of his tongue plated with her clit before he flattened it with the flat side. Unlike their first time in his chair, Night didn't fool around or tease her. His tongue swirled while his lips sucked and slurped, pulling at her sensitive flesh. Under her clit, he made long jerky moves that had Trinity's hips bucking. As she came, she yanked on Night's locks, melting on both the outside and the inside. He sucked up her juices and looked up at her, eyes ablaze yet again. He crawled up her body slowly, a predator who'd captured his prey and ready to feast. Trinity was trying to capture her breath from the rousing orgasm he'd just given her. He was naked on top of her, that length that drove her crazy easing it's way between her folds. Night reached above her and unsnapped her legs from the binds on the headboard. Her legs fell around his hips just as he penetrated her. He held himself up on his elbows, sliding into her so effortlessly as if they'd been together for years. He tilted his head forward, resting his forehead on top of hers.

His first stroke stole her breath away. She gasped and closed her eyes for a moment, the pleasure of his stroke making her lose control. When she opened her eyes, she found Night's deep chocolate pools gazing at her. For the first time, Trinity could actually see the depth of his age in the reflection of his eyes. He looked no more than her own age, but through his eyes, Trinity saw years, decades, hell, even centuries.

"So beautiful," Night muttered as Trinity gasped from his change of tempo, his thrusts coming in with a touch of speed and strength, impacting her in the way she needed it to. He kissed her open mouth. Trinity wrapped her legs around him tightly, not wanting to be anywhere else but here. Not only that, but she felt a heavy protectiveness swarming her heart. As Night made love to her insides, deep enough to bulge her stomach, Trinity couldn't see herself with another man. She couldn't imagine clutching onto another man as hard as she was clutching onto Night, begging for more. In that same manner, she would be ready to kill any woman who wanted him. Her body, her mind, even her heart claimed the man that she felt immense protection and pleasure from. His thickness surging repeatedly; knocking on her g-spot, the way he growled and grunted, all the way to how her pussy gurgled and sucked him inside of her; it all belonged to her. He belonged to her.

"You're all mine now," Trinity grunted. She bit his lips and clenched her muscles, squeezing him within her.

"I'll all yours," he growled, his thrusts becoming chaotic.

"And you don't ever need another woman Night. I'm all you need!"

"Fuck! Trinity your pussy is so damn good," he breathed.

"Can you handle another bite my love?" he asked. Through the dark, Trinity could see the whiteness of his sharp fangs.

"Take it," she moaned. She turned her head to the side to bare her neck. Unlike the other bites, this one was ravenous and as crazed as his strokes. The sharp ends of his teeth tore through her skin. Trinity screamed out, the pain rocking her core. But just as the pain came, it dulled, the soft pulling motions he made easing her pain away. Her body shuddered, creaming on his dick as she came. In that instant, Trinity felt something snap tight inside of her as if there was a missing part of her that was finally found. She suddenly felt the pleasure it gave Night to suck her blood, she felt the intensity of his own orgasm as his body stuttered on top of her. Before, Trinity was able to sense his feelings, as if she could tap into his essence, but now it was even clearer. She felt something shift within her own body. It was as if, having his essence be part of her made her stronger, sharper. She didn't realize how much of her had been missing until Night made her whole.

He slipped out of her body and fell next to her. The sound of ragged breathing filled the room, as they tried to compose themselves. Night felt the essence that belonged to Trinity firmly wrap tight around his heart and seal itself there, cementing Trinity as his mate. They'd both shown and proven that they wanted each other beyond the measures of simple desires. The bond had cemented into place on those terms, feeling just how drawn to each other they were. Trinity turned and looked at him, laying on her side. Night did the same. He pushed a wild curl from her face.

"I've always wanted to cut it. But my family would never let me live that down," Trinity sighed.

"You're beautiful no matter what Trinity. And those people aren't your family anymore. Not the way they treat you," he replied. He rested his arm over her hips and pulled her closer to him.

"Night..." her words trailed off as she thought about what she was going to say.

"What is it darling?" he asked.

"You've lived a long time. Have there ever been another woman that you-"

"Let that not worry you Trinity. I have had only one love before. She was sweet, caring, full of life and loved to laugh. I was very smitten with her and I wanted to spend all my time with her. That didn't last of course. 100 years later, I run into someone like you. Bull headed, strong, sassy, and so damned cute. Vampires are sexual creatures darling, but once we've set our eyes on a woman, that's pretty much it. We take joy in chasing that particular woman and not getting distracted by others. Don't think that because I've lived a long time that this is some fling. I said I wanted you and I very well mean that."

With the newfound sensations inside of her, Trinity felt the truth in his words.

"Turn me, Night," she said. His eyes flashed gold before returning to normal.

"I can't," he stated.

"But—but why? You just said you wanted me."

"And I do. But turning you only has two results. Failure or success. We can be together without you being turned Trinity."

"How?!"

"Because I drink from you, and we are connected, if you take small amounts of my blood your natural lifespan will increase to match mine."

"Humans can't breakdown the enzymes in blood." Trinity said.

"Trust me darling, you will be able to handle my blood. It wouldn't be any more than a small amount anyways. Anything too large can kill you. You trust me right?" Night asked.

"I do," Trinity replied without hesitation.

"But what about..." *Babies.* Trinity wanted to say that the only way she could mother his children was if she was a vampire too, but she swallowed the words. No sense in bringing up such talk like that when they had other issues to deal with.

"You're sad," Night said. It wasn't a question. He could feel it.

"I just for once want my life to be the way I want it to be. No questions asked, no rules, just life being lived. Just me, being happy," Trinity said.

"Oh? And I don't make you happy?" Night asked. His nose shifted back and forth until it turned into the snout of a pig. Trinity covered her mouth as she snorted with her laugher.

"Are you really telling me that I don't make you happy?!" His nose snorted as he made oinking sounds, nuzzling her neck. Trinity burst out laughing as he tickled her with his wet nose.

"Alright, alright! You make me happy!" Trinity laughed.

She clutched her stomach as tears leaked from her eyes. Night moved away and returned his nose to normal.

"Wow," he sighed.

"What?" she questioned, catching her breath.

"You're so beautiful when your smile touches your eyes," he replied. Her laugher died down, but her smile never left her face. Although he had turned down her request to change her, it didn't take away from the fact that she wanted to be with him. Plus, he was giving her a chance to be with him forever in time. She wouldn't age normally and she would be able to last years without slowing down. It would just be them.

"Well, I've never seen a sexy black man with a pig's snout," Trinity smiled.

"But seriously, I feel natural with you. Normal. I guess that makes my smiles genuine," she said. She rose up and pushed him onto his back, then mounted his hips.

"You've had me under your mercy this whole time. Now, it's time for you to be under mine," she threatened, eager to take him within her body again and ride until his toes were curling.

Chapter Sixteen

NIGHT FELT THE SUN ACROSS HIS FACE BUT HE DIDN'T want to move. Not with Trinity's soft body against his. Her bare breasts were squished against his chest from where she had fallen from on top of him. Last night was the best night of his life. Even when he had nights with his beloved, this particular night with Trinity was the night that his whole life seemed to start over. Waking up with her essence throbbing through him, able to feel her every emotion so clearly like it was his own spirit inside of him.

He couldn't help but run his hands over her smooth skin. When she'd asked to be turned, a flicker of fear had shot through him. He was able to make it through losing his beloved, but Trinity was his mate. His true mate. If he ever lost her, he too was going to be lost. He couldn't trust the odds of the bite against her life. He wasn't going to do it this time.

Trinity moaned slightly as she began to stir. She stretched out on top of him and yawned. She snuggled into his chest as his locks surrounded her like a blanket.

"You feel so good," she mumbled, wiggling on top of him. Night chuckled and kissed her forehead.

"As do you darling," he replied. Trinity picked her head up

and looked at him, a small smile touching her face. She was just so cute, her hair tousled, her eyes squinty with sleep and her lips pouty.

"You've got a little drool," he laughed, wiping the corner of her mouth. Trinity yelped and hopped off of him immediately, wiping at her face.

"How embarrassing!" she squealed. Night just laughed at her and watched her ass jiggle as she ran into the bathroom. He slowly got out of the bed, also naked. She'd left the bathroom door opened, so he just entered after her. She was sitting on the toilet humming. Night smiled at her as he stood in front of the sink to brush his teeth. She watched in awe as he brushed his human teeth first and then switched out his toothbrush for one catered specific to his fangs. He brushed then flossed, then rinsed with mouthwash. When he was done, he opened the door to the shower and cut it on. Trinity couldn't keep her eyes off him, one because she was smitten, and two because he was sexy as fuck and his long dick was just hanging around. She couldn't help but stare.

While the water heated, he opened the closet door and pulled out an unopened toothbrush. He waved it at her then left it on the counter so she knew it was hers to use. Then, he was slipping in the shower. Trinity wanted to see the way the water cascaded all around him. Maybe she might dip to her knees and pull his thick flesh into her mouth. Cursing, Trinity wiped herself and then flushed the toilet. She brushed her teeth diligently, before she was opening the shower door. Night was stroking himself with soap, effectively cleaning his dick. He didn't look surprised to see her entering. He just moved over to allow her entry before wrapping her in his arms and kissing on her.

"I could wake up like this every morning," Night said. True, Trinity felt the same. These were the types of mornings she always wished she could have. Instead, she'd had overbearing parents and ignorant ass Trent.

Their shower was wild and hot but even with the sexual energy between them, they didn't have sex. What they had was shared intimacy, touching, kissing, laughing and embracing each other. That was the true nature of their budding relationship. Trinity was head over heels.

"I usually go to the kitchen and then eat breakfast with some of my clan members, but I can just bring something up for you to eat," Night told her as they finished dressing from their shower. He'd had one of the female vampires in his clan do some shopping for Trinity and bought her an array of clothing. From just her touch he knew her sizes and because he was now sharing such a connection with her, he knew what she would like.

"Don't be silly Night. I can come downstairs and eat with you and the clan too." She flounced her hair over her shoulder and headed towards the door. She walked away without him and Night had to snap from his daze to catch up to her. She was full of surprises that woman was.

Night was used to being greeted by his clan, but when he saw them greeting Trinity with respect and accepting her into the fold, his heart stopped thumping nervously. This wasn't like other supernatural hierarchies. A clan leader's mate would be respected but they didn't hold the power the clan leader did. That meant that the clan could reject the mate if they didn't feel safe or that it was a proper choice. Night had seen many clan leader step down from their positions because their clan did not approve of their mate. In most circumstances, clans have good reason for rejecting a mate, and Trinity being human could have been one of those good reasons.

Instead, his clan embraced her with open arms. Even the children were surrounding her in their curiosity, pulling on her hair softly and staring at her teeth wondering when she would have fangs.

"When can we expect a baby?" Blaze asked, sneaking up behind Night. Night waved him away not even wanting to entertain that idea again. When he'd spoken to Trinity about it, he assumed she was just curious. But what if she really did want children? If they were destined to be together forever, she wouldn't be able to have his babes until he turned her. It made Night anxious just thinking about it.

For the rest of the morning, the clan enjoyed a large breakfast in the dining room of the club. Night sat next to Trinity, his arms around her, feeling as if they'd done this over a thousand times already. Trinity was equally comfortable, laughing and talking with the clan as if she'd always been a part of the family.

Once breakfast had been eaten, and the dining tables cleared, the clan went off in their own ways, fulfilling their own agendas for the day. Night retreated to his office with Trinity behind him. She had gone quiet and her eyes were distant. He felt and saw that she was deeply thinking.

"You want to go back," he said. Feeling the conflict she had with staying at the club and going back home to her parents.

"I need to handle something," she sighed.

"Then we'll both go," Night declared.

"No, Night. I need to do this alone. I need them to hear me and realize that I'm not going to settle anymore. Plus, there had to be a way out of that contract. I haven't found it yet so I have a few things to take care of. But I'll be back tonight. I won't sleep in another bed that's not yours Night." Even though he was against it, Night knew he had to let her do what she must. He took her hands and kissed the back of them.

"I'll miss you," he whispered.

"Me too." She tilted her head back and puckered her lips, making kissing sounds. Night chuckled as he leaned down and kissed her soft lips.

"You'd better leave before I get carried away," he warned.

"I'm leaving," she sang.

"Wait. Take this." Night went to his office desk and pulled her phone from the drawer. He had turned it off after it kept ringing from Trent's call. He held no importance in Trinity's life and Night was not going to allow him to weigh her down with his bullshit.

He gave her the cell phone and watched as she turned it on. Her eyes lit up with the amount of messages and missed calls that began to come through. She shook her head and sighed.

"This is going to be rough," she mumbled as she looked at the messages.

"I'll be back soon, Night," she said, not even looking at him. Right in that moment Night knew that something wasn't right. His gut began to churn and blare with warning but still, he didn't stop Trinity from leaving.

"YES." Just before Trinity arrived to her parents' home, her phone was going off again. She answered this time without looking at the screen.

"You have severely upset us Trinity," her father's voice was calm but she sensed his anger.

"We need to speak," she said.

"Damn right we do. We're all at Trent's home. Join us. Now." The line went dead. She'd taken a cab from Night's club and the driver was a vampire. He pulled up to Trent's home after Trinity gave him the new address. He turned around and looked at her.

"Night has not been in love like this for a long time. We have accepted you because we see the positive change in Night. We feel your genuineness to our kind. Whatever problems that await you here will not await you in vamp town. Don't be afraid to come back to us no matter how much you a threatened. We will fight for you if need be, Trinity," he declared. She bowed her head at him, the honesty in his words making her heart leap. She nearly wanted to cry. She didn't like that she had to come back to this place to talk and fight for her freedom this way. She just wanted to have it.

"I'm coming back. No matter what I have to do. This isn't my life. A future with Night is all I want," she admitted. He smiled at her and nodded.

"I'll tell Night I dropped you off safely. Call me if you need me to pick you back up and Night is busy," he said.

"I will," Trinity smiled as she scooted out of his car. The front gates to Trent's home was looming in front of her like something from a nightmare.

The gates creaked open slowly. Trinity took a deep breath and walked the large circular driveway towards to front door. The moment she approached, the door was opened for her. Vickie smiled glumly at her as Trinity walked by. She motioned towards the parlor. Like something out of some creepy Stepford wives scene, her parents, her sister and Trent were sitting in the parlor, still as stone. Occasionally, her mother would bring a small teacup to her lips and sip. When Trinity entered, all eyes slowly came to her.

"I take it the dinner party sucked?" Trinity smirked. Humor was the only thing that was going to hide her distress.

"Do you think this is some joke?" her father snapped.

"We were all embarrassed! We've had to tell everyone you were sick and watch as they gave us looks of disbelief! They think you've really run off and we're just trying to save face. The whole night was an embarrassment and you come in here laughing?"

"I already told you all that I didn't want this. So if you're embarrassed, that's not my problem," Trinity shrugged. Trent cleared his throat and looked at her but he didn't speak.

"What part of contractually obligated you don't understand?" Her mother asked.

"Not only that, but everyone is whispering that this marriage won't happen and you're a rebel and we're losing our power over town. You're ruining this for all of us Trinity! Don't you care about your own family?"

"Family? The family that doesn't listen to me? The family that forces me to marry a man I don't love? The family that fucks said man behind my back? The family that thinks all this shit is normal? No, I don't care about my own family. Not anymore. I'm tired of living a life for what other people think. If Trent and Tracee can so easily fuck each other, then they can easily marry each other. I already told you that. She's always wanted my life we all know that. So, give it to her," Trinity said.

"You're so quick to point out who I fucked, but you haven't uttered a word about who you're fucking," Trent stated. His voice was low and deep, his anger being held back, barely. He sipped his scotch and turned towards her.

"People saw you with that vampire Trinity. And once they realized you were not at this dinner party, even through our excuses we heard whispers about you sneaking off with that vampire."

"If you want me to admit it, I have no problem with that. I've been fucking a vampire. A vampire who cares about me actually. A vampire who definitely fucks better than you can. Are you happy now?" Trent just glared at her. He squeezed the arms of the chair as if trying to keep his anger in check.

"That vampire doesn't care about you. You're so damn easy he just keeps coming back because he doesn't have to put in any effort to fuck you. No one will ever truly love you Trinity because you don't fucking listen. I tried to make an honest woman out of you and you can't even let that happen. I would never want a woman like you carrying my last name or my children. You'll shame us all. Even though the contract is set in stone, I'm going to bypass certain clauses. I will marry your sister, who is clearly the better choice. She listens and she caters to my needs. It will be easy to generate a story about finding true love through her than with someone like you," Trent said. She didn't know what reaction they wanted her to have but Trinity was relieved. It felt as if someone had finally shoved air into her lungs and she could breathe.

"Great choice Trent," Trinity said. "I guess then, I will just leave."

"No," he objected.

"No?" she asked.

"Sit down and have tea with us. I'm having someone come and take pictures so it looks like we're one happy family. I'll use these photos as my Segway to my marriage with Tracee. The least you can do is help us close this awful chapter so a new one can start with me and Tracee," he answered. Trinity wanted nothing more than to just leave and rush into Night's arms, but if she was being let out of this stupid contract and given her freedom, taking these pictures was truly the least she could do. She wouldn't have to hear from Trent again.

"Alright. Fine. I'll take the pictures," she agreed. Trent nodded but said nothing more. The parlor went eerily quiet as Vickie pushed out the cart for tea and biscuits. She left then, and it was her mother who stood and began pouring out each cup of tea and adding a biscuit to each small plate.

"You finally got your wish after all," her mother said, handing Trinity her cup of tea. They were all saddened, but Trinity refused to feel guilty.

"We all make our sacrifices I suppose," Trinity replied. Her mother sat down and began drinking her tea in silence. Trinity watched as they all sipped their tea, pretending that this was some normal affair. Then again, this was the life of rich people here. Trinity sighed and took a few gulps of her own tea. It was sweet like she liked it so she didn't mind drinking more than half of it.

"When is the photographer coming?" Trinity asked. Trent looked at his watch.

"In five minutes. I told him the importance of time and with the amount I'm paying him I'm sure he'll make sure to be on time," Trent said.

"Paying off someone usually makes them do what you want," Trinity said.

"Not everyone. You would have had the world at your feet and a never-ending scope of money. Yet still, you refused."

"Money doesn't buy happiness," she stated.

"But it does make people do crazy shit," he said. He put his teacup down and stood.

"A vampire huh? Over me? The richest bachelor in Louisiana," Trent sighed. Trinity opened her mouth to speak. Trent swung his arm, backhanding her hard. The sting of the slap echoed through her entire face as she was thrown from her chair. Her teacup went flying, and shattered on the ground.

"You bitch," Trinity coughed, spitting out blood from her busted lip. She hoisted herself from the ground and looked around, realizing that neither of her parents and not even her sister was shocked at what Trent had done. They sat there, sipping their tea as if they were blind.

"You'd let him hit me?!" Trinity screeched. No one answered her.

"Fuck this!" Trinity jumped off the floor, whirling around to land a punch in Trent's face. She clawed his neck and kicked at him, defending her own honor for him having the nerve to slap her. He pushed her away from him and backhanded her again. Trinity's eyes crossed from the force of the slap as she fell to the ground once more. A searing pain rolled across her stomach. She grabbed at her stomach.

"Ugh! What the fuck?!" she screamed. She began to cough, feeling as if something was caught in her throat.

"It's called jimsonweed. The basic shrub but it's dangerous if ingested at high quantities. Isn't hard to find and not easily detectable," Trent shrugged.

"What?" Trinity coughed.

"You really thought that I would just let you walk out of here? After the way you embarrassed me? I will gratefully marry your sister and she will be the perfect wife. But people are discrediting me because they think I'm using excuses to hide the fact that you're running around with a damn vampire. I told them you were sick, and now they'll believe me. The photographer will take pictures of your sickly body. Only, your sickness would have led you to die. We'll all grieve and eventually I will find comfort in your sister who I then fall in love with. People will be so happy I'm not torn up by your death that they'll be eager to attend our new wedding and give us well wishes. And you, you'll just be a memory and unable to stain my life or your parents' life," Trent explained. Trinity coughed harder, feeling as if her lungs were being squeezed.

"No one gets one over on me. I always get what I want. And since you don't want to live the life I would have provided you Trinity, you don't get to live at all," he chuckled. Trinity turned and tried to crawl away. She reached out to her parents, in attempt to get them to help her.

"You've left us no choice Trinity," her mother stated.

"It was either this, or we would lose everything. Our house. Our money. Our legacy. You were right. Sacrifices do have to be made. Today, we're all making one," her father said. They stood and just looked down at her. Tracee also stood, and walked over to their parents, standing in front of them. She was smirking smugly as she watched Trinity convulse and cough on the ground.

"She'll be dead in less than three minutes," Trent informed them. A shrill scream erupted in the room.

"What are you doing?!" Vickie screamed.

"Someone get some help!" She rushed towards Trinity, falling to the ground next to her.

"Do something!" she screamed at Trent. No one moved. When it dawned on her that they had all planned this, Vickie's eyes went wide. She grabbed Trinity under the arms and began dragging Trinity away, knowing no one there was going to help her.

"Is she going to go to the cops? Should we do something?!" James exclaimed. Trent groaned and followed after Vickie who could only move so quickly. He grabbed Vickie by the back of the head and jerked her back. With one punch, her body went lax, knocking her out.

"James. Help me." Trent picked Trinity up who was still coughing violently, carrying her through to the back of the house. James followed, with Vickie in his arms. Outside in the backyard, Trent dumped Trinity to the concrete floor of the garage. Vickie's body plopped down, her eyes closed. Trinity tried to reach to her, but her stomach cramped as her coughs became violent. Her body began to shake uncontrollably. She was only able to pull in one more gasp of air as her eyes rolled to the back of her head and foam bubbled up in her mouth.

Night. Help me. Trinity registered those three words of consciousness before her heart seized and froze entirely, beating no more.

Chapter Seventeen

ANGER. NIGHT FELT IT SWIRLING AROUND IN HIS BODY but it wasn't coming from him. He knew immediately it was Trinity's anger. Night sighed hard, a deep groan leaving his mouth. Blaze looked up from where he was seated across from Night at his desk. Both of them were surrounded by paperwork but Night couldn't concentrate.

"Trinity?" Blaze asked.

"She's angry," Night sighed.

"She's with her parents. Of course she's angry," Blaze shrugged.

"True but I'm just—I'm uneasy about all of this. I should have gone with her despite what she said," Night said.

"And that would undermine her ability to speak for herself and to take back her life. Trinity's headstrong, she needs this to feel completely free from her parents. You hovering and protecting her won't give her the feeling that she handled it on her own. Besides she would admit that she needs you if she did for this," Blaze assured him. Night sat back to think.

"We have a lot of work to do here Night. All these contracts to look over plus all the money being shelled out for feedings, we need to keep track of the books right now. Trinity can handle herself, okay? And she would hate to come back and see that you still have all this work to do. If I know mates, I know the minute she comes back, you're gonna be sniffing at her panties, wanting to fuck her repeatedly. But you're not gonna be able to do that until we finish this work. Now. Let's work." Night smirked knowing he was going to do that exact same thing.

"Alright," Night smiled. Night held his head down and continued to work, doing his best to focus on the contracts that lay in front of him.

Anxiousness. Frustration. Weariness. Relief. Night felt all of Trinity's emotions rolling through him. When that relief poured through him, he sighed in content, happy that Trinity had a moment of relief. That something had happened to make her finally achieve of sense of relief.

"She's done it. She's figured out this whole situation," Night revealed. Blaze looked at him.

"See, I told you she would handle it! We've gotten through most of these bills and contracts, I think we can take a small break. I'll get us something from the bar." Blaze stood, gathering some of the papers together before leaving the office with them in his hands. Night sighed again and closed his eyes.

"Hurry back Trinity. I miss you," he whispered to himself, wishing Trinity could hear him. He wanted to feel her kinky coils in his fingers, her body heat against his body, the touch of her soft lips against his. She was so witty and fun, Night could only imagine how their lives would mesh together. He couldn't wait to start living again with her. His heart burned with desperation. He missed her too fucking much.

Distress. Night became alert, the moment the feeling of relief halted. He slowly began to stand. What was wrong with her? Why would she be feeling distressed?

Fear. Panic.

"No! Trinity, what's the matter?!" Night spoke to himself, beginning to panic himself.

Pain. That did it for Night. He rushed out from behind his desk, nearly tripping over his own chair. He shot down the hall and jumped the flight of stairs, using his supernatural speed and agility. He landed on club level in a squat.

"I was just coming back," Blaze said with two drinks in his hands.

"Trinity. Something is wrong. Deadly wrong," Night stated evenly. His stomach began to churn. His lungs squeezed with phantom pain, feeling as if he couldn't breathe. It wasn't his pain. Someone was hurting his Trinity. And he was going to kill them.

"We need to go. Now!" Night shouted, the pain in his body rising immensely. Night's eyes became fiery red, the panic of something harming his mate fusing with anger of someone harming his mate.

Night stormed from the club, barely touching the stairs leading up to the entryway before the magic of his large raven was taking over his body. Night took to the sky, squawking as he jetted towards his mate. Below him, Blaze powered up his motorcycle and rode behind Night who disappeared into the sky.

Like an internal GPS, Night was able to follow the link he had inside of himself to Trinity. He could feel the change of her heartbeat and at first it was fluttering with adrenaline but now it was slow, as if she was getting tired. The raven squawked, flapping its wings harder and jetting through the sky. Night came upon the large gates from where he could sense Trinity's faint essence behind it. He didn't care who's human house this was, he was going to get his damn mate and rip everyone else to shreds. Night landed on the top of the gate and waited for the roar of Blaze's bike that was only a minute away. Blaze jumped off the bike. He grasped onto the gate and climbed it easily, moving quickly up the structure. Night jumped from the top of the gate as a raven but landed on the lawn behind the gate as a man. He closed his eyes to calm his racing heart. Trinity's essence was a sharp color of violet that wove around his heart like string. He saw the path of the violet string like a leash leading Night straight to Trinity.

"This way," Night said to Blaze. Night walked intently around the large circular driveway towards the side of the house. The mansion would intimidate anyone, but Night didn't give a damn who caught him walking the property. There was another side gate leading to a large section of the house that looked like the garage.

Night. Help me. Night felt his heart stutter and come to a full stop, ceasing to beat. He grabbed his chest, bending over as he tried to catch his breath.

"What's wrong?!" Blaze exclaimed.

"Trinity. She's dead," he gasped out. Night tore open the gate in front of him, falling over as he ran through it. He brushed dirt and grass stains from his body as he scrambled to his feet and ran to the large garage.

Blaze kneeled and pulled up the garage door, breaking the mechanical chains that made the door operate with a remote. Night darted under the door when there was barely enough room for him to fit but he didn't care.

He heard the scream that left his mouth and it truly didn't even sound like his own. He crawled to Trinity and scooped her into his arms. She had foamed at the mouth as if someone had poisoned her.

"Please don't. Please don't Trinity. Not when I just found you," he wept, brushing her hair from her face. Her eyes were in the back of her head, her body stiff but still warm.

"No," Blaze breathed, finally seeing Trinity's body. Night's eyes began to glow deep orange, the violet strings of Trinity's essence that was wrapped around his heart beginning to disintegrate. His fangs dipped from his gums. Pain seared through him, making him grit his teeth.

"Night. No!" Blaze shouted, seeing Night struggle with the urge to become rogue.

"They. Killed. My. Heart," Night growled, his nails lengthening. His breathing was hoarse and labored, his vision hazing over with a red hue.

"I'll kill everyone in sight," he threatened, his voice unrecognizable in his partly rogue state.

A large burst of light filled the garage. Both Blaze and Night covered their eyes, the flash almost too much for their sensitive visions.

"Cut it out!" The soft shrill of a voice was one that Night would never forget. He lifted his head, despite the glare of the light. His beloved was sitting directly in front of him, her brows furrowed, her lips sealed to a tight line. Night clutched onto Trinity and just glared at the woman he had once loved, the woman he would always love but now he had a woman who he would love even more.

"Stop the urge to be rogue Night," she ordered. Night felt his eyes burn with tears as he held Trinity.

"She's different," Night said.

"I know she is. I told you, I'll always be with you. And I know who this woman is. And because of who she is, you need to do something about it. Before it's too late. Get yourself together Night and do what you have to do!" she demanded.

"You were afraid to change her because she would die like I did, but at this point she's already dead. She can't get any more dead than this. Do it!" Night looked down at Trinity. Her lips were beginning to turn blue. He took her wrist and looked at her dimming vein.

"Maybe I can still change her," Night told Blaze.

"Do it!" Blaze urged. Night wasted no more time, biting into her wrist, as deep as he could. Her body involuntarily jerked. He tasted the poison that was laced into her blood. He kept sucking, drinking the poison just as he drank her blood. His supernatural DNA allowed for him to consume the poison and heal himself quick enough not to be affected by it. With her being dead and Night trying to change her, he had to just about drain her blood from her body, eliminating what killed her in the first place. However, drinking blood of an adult human in its entirety was too much for any vampire. Night felt himself struggling with control, that savage part of him surfacing on bloodlust.

Help me, brother. Night projected his thoughts into Blaze. Blaze swooped over and took Trinity's other wrist. He bit down and began drinking her blood, draining her from the poison inside of her. Both vampires fed off of her, taking the poison into their bodies until there was nothing left. Blaze unlatched his fangs. It was Night's duty to illicit the change. With Blaze unlatched from her, Night shuddered as he released his venom into Trinity's body. His body naturally released as much venom as needed for the change to suit the body of the human that was being changed. Darkness threatened to fall over Night when his venom was deposited into the bite, as his body got weak. His fangs ejected from Trinity's skin. He fell away from her, trying to catch his breath. Grogginess corrupted his mind, something that would take over after a feeding and a changing bite this potent. Something cold brushed against his cheek. He lifted his lowered lids slightly. His beloved was glowing in front of him, her ghostly figure cold.

"I won't let you lose her Night," she told him. Night was confused, not understanding what she would be able to do to save Trinity if the bite didn't work. Before he could ask however, her ghostly figure slid away from him. Night watched as she smiled at him then looked at Trinity and dove into her body.

"I couldn't see her, but I suppose the only spirit that would follow you around is her. Was that who was just here?" Blaze asked. Night just nodded.

"I want to kill these people for doing this to Trinity, but we have to think about her now. This isn't a safe place for her and after giving her the changing bite you will be weakened." Night clenched his fists and nodded.

"And this human, we have to leave her. She isn't our business," Blaze said, nodding towards the older woman who was laying limply by Trinity. She was knocked out cold, but she wasn't dead.

"Fly back and I will ride with Trinity on my bike." Blaze scooped Trinity carefully into his arms, knowing that if he didn't handle with care, Night would become vicious against him.

"I don't want to leave her," Night grumbled, feeling the weakness overcoming him.

"The faster we move, the faster you'll have her in your arms. Come on. We can go to Emma's home. It's closer than the club. Let's go Night." In moments like these, Night was thankful for having a level headed friend that would fight for Night no matter the circumstances.

Night closed his eyes, imagining feathers overtaking his body. He used his magic, changing into his large raven with a grunt. Seeing that he had made the change, Blaze left the garage with Trinity in his arms, moving with vampire speed that no human would be able to track. To them, it would be nothing more than a blur. Night flew out of the garage, above Blaze, watching as he cradled Trinity while he climbed the large gate again and then straddled his bike. Trinity had not opened her eyes or moved an inch. Night just prayed the bite worked this time. It had to work.

EMMA SCREAMED when a large bird came flying into her house. It burst through her front door, falling to the ground as if it was too tired to fly any longer. It's size had Emma running and ducking for cover. Black dust puffed from the ground, making Emma peek out from behind the couch where she was hiding. She saw the flow of long locks and deep chocolate skin.

"Night?!" She exclaimed. Through her front door, Blaze kicked opened the door that had closed slightly after the bird forced its way through. Blaze was carrying a limp Trinity in his arms.

"What the hell happened?!" Emma gasped. "Bring her in here!" Emma led the way to the guest room so Blaze could put Trinity to lay down on the bed. He carefully set her down after Emma pulled back the covers. Once Trinity was comfortable on the bed, Blaze left the room without saying anything. Emma was confused, tears beginning to sting her eyes when she touched Trinity's wrist and felt no pulse.

Blaze had left the bedroom to help his best friend. Night was too weakened to move from the kitchen floor. He pulled Night to his feet, putting his arm around Night's waist and helping him walk into the bedroom. By the time they reached the bedroom. Night was barely conscious. Blaze set Night on the bed next to Trinity, pushing Night close enough so he could feel Trinity against him. Night nuzzled her neck before he fell into a deep sleep.

"We should get her to the hospital Blaze. She's not breathing!" Emma sniffled, continuing to try and search for a pulse.

"No. Leave her be," Blaze replied, his voice hard.

"I don't understand," Emma whispered.

"She was poisoned. I'm guessing either her family or the man she was set to marry was the one who did it. She was trying to get out of whatever they were holding her to. Apparently, they couldn't settle with her just leaving so they resorted to just trying to kill her."

"What do we do? We can't just leave her like this."

"When me and Night found her, her heart already stopped beating. Night and I drank her blood and then Night infected her with his venom," Blaze explained.

"Wait. Does that mean...does that mean she's going to turn into a vampire?" Emma asked.

"In retrospect, yes. But the changing bite isn't 100 percent successful. You either change, or you die. There's no in between. Trinity was already dead when Night changed her so we're hoping that it can be reversed. Especially because we drank the poison from her body."

"What happened to Night?"

"When vampires release their venom it makes them weak. Changing Trinity because she was already dead was even more taxing on him. Sleep helps him heal. Right now all we can do is wait. Trinity will either wake, or she won't." Emma hugged herself tightly, looking at the way Night was cuddling against Trinity. Blaze reached over to Emma and took her into his arms, holding her tightly as he sensed her need to be comforted.

"It's hard to just wait, I know," Blaze said, kissing her temple.

"I just can't imagine a life without her. She's family."

"I know what you mean. I don't want to lose Night either. We share a blood bond. I would feel completely lost without him," Blaze sighed.

"Why would you lose Night?" Blaze cleared his throat and rubbed the stubble on his jaw against Emma's cheek.

"Night and Trinity share what we call a mate bond. You can fall in love with anyone but you truly only form a mate bone with one person. Ever. Forming that mate bond literally changes you. They're connected to each other in a way that's deeper than just emotions. It's physical, it's mental. If Trinity dies, Night won't survive it. The loss would just be too much. It would just literally kill him."

"Wow. I didn't know how serious this was. I just want both of them to survive." Emma looked up at Blaze, seeing his deep concern.

"You've never found your true mate?" Emma asked him quietly.

"No, I haven't." Blaze knew the moment he said it, that it was the wrong thing to say. Emma pulled away from him and went towards the bed. She fiddled around with the sheets to make sure Trinity was comfortable.

"Em," he called out. She ignored him.

"Don't ignore me, my sweet Em."

"I'm just really concerned about Trinity," she said, trying to deflect.

"I care about you Emma. Deeply. I crave you more than I should but I just do. When I don't see you I drive myself crazy thinking about you. Don't think that you're just a means to an end for me because you're not," Blaze told her. Emma exhaled. She took in his words, but she didn't reply. But her expression let Blaze know she heard everything he said.

"How long will this take?"

"If she doesn't wake by tomorrow morning, she won't ever wake," Blaze replied, his voice daunting.

"Wake up, Trinity." The soft voice was a caress against Trinity's ear. She yawned and stretched.

"I'm awake," she grumbled, not attempting to move. *Whap!* The sting of a slap fell across Trinity's face. Trinity jumped up, holding her face. Her eyes landed on a woman she'd never seen before.

"Did you just fucking slap me?!" Trinity shouted at her.

"I told you to get up," she replied easily. Trinity drew her hand back.

"Don't you dare!" the woman exclaimed.

"Give me a good reason I shouldn't slap you back?" Trinity asked her.

"Because I'm going to get you back to Night," she said.

"Night?" Trinity looked around. For the first time she noticed that she didn't recognize where she was. She couldn't even really say where she was. Thick fog only allowed her to see directly in front of her. Then it all came back to her in a rush. Trent. Her parents. Her sister. Poison. Death.

"Is this hell?" Trinity asked, realizing she had truly died.

"Because if I'm a demon you better believe I'm gonna

torment my family for doing this shit to me," Trinity added. The woman laughed vibrantly.

"Oh no! Don't be silly child. Your heart is much too genuine for hell. You're a firecracker and Night will have his hands full with you, but you don't deserve such dreadful circumstances. Besides, Night needs a woman like you."

"But my family poisoned me! I died!"

"And Night gave you the changing bite. At this very moment his venom is pumping through your body. All you have to do is wake and accept the change."

"He did?! I thought he never would. I wanted to be a vampire before all of this. Wait, how do you know so much?"

"I've been watching. I told Night I would look after him. I would never just leave him until he was able to find happiness again. And he has. With you."

"Are you...are you the one he tried to change?" Trinity asked, realizing this woman must have been the reason Night had been afraid to turn her. The woman only nodded grimly. She was saddened for a moment, but then her eyes brightened with delight.

"I have not been able to move on because I can't just leave Night. But now, because I know he has you Trinity, I can finally move on. You need to wake up. Accept the bite," she said.

"But how?" Trinity asked.

"Why did you want to be a vampire?" she asked.

"Because I wanted to be with Night. Because being with Night made me happy. Being in his world; it was different but it was opposite everything that I've been forced to live. Night lets me be myself. And well, my body my heart, I just can't stay away from him," Trinity explained.

"You are bonded with him. I know you feel it," she said. Trinity nodded in agreement.

"Follow the bond Trinity. Feel the bond. And then just

wake up." Trinity just stared at the woman, unsure of what the hell she was supposed to do. The woman reached out with two fingers, pressing them over Trinity's eyes. She closed Trinity's lids, and Trinity understood that the woman wanted Trinity to look within herself by closing her eyes.

Trinity exhaled sharply but she kept her eyes closed. *Night, where are you?* She asked herself. Follow the bond. What did that mean? Searching for Night made Trinity think about the man that turned her life on its head in the best of ways. Images of Night's smile, the way his locks swayed against his naked body when they were together. How her heart fluttered when he held her in his warm embrace. The timbre of his voice when he whispered against her ear. Trinity shuddered every time she thought about it. And now, she just wanted to be captured in his arms again, feeling their hearts beat in the same rhythm because they would be the same species. A burst of velvety indigo smoke clouded around Trinity's mind. She had no idea what it was, and how she was even seeing it, but she didn't open her eyes and ruin the vision. The smoke swirled and moved gently, forming into thin vines. She used her mind to follow the lines the vines were making. Following those vines, she felt the closest to Night. She could sense his grief, that resided deep within his fatigue.

Don't be upset, Night. Trinity's heart bled, feeling that type of pain within Night. Her mind moved faster, following the winding roads of vines that spread through her body, entangling with the colors of her own spirit. Just as she reached the end of the vine, she saw Night. His eyes were closed but his brows were furrowed. His pain was deep, and emotional and not even his sleep could help ease it.

I'll ease your pain. Trinity said the words. She wasn't even sure if it was aloud or in her own mind. She tipped forward and imagined herself touching Night.

The world tumbled out from her and she slipped away

from solid ground. Her entire body seized with pain as her veins went up in flames. She burned from the inside out, her body contorting as she tried to regain control of herself. What felt like pinpricks all over her body made Trinity squeal in pain. Her body shook violently before everything as she knew it simply went dark.

***

GASPING FOR AIR, Trinity shot up from the bed. She clutched at her throat, feeling as if she couldn't breathe. Her vision was hazed over. She blinked a couple of times before her vision zoomed in and became sharper. Her gums were aching as she tried to catch her breath. She didn't have to look around. One inhale and she knew she was in Emma's guest bedroom. She could smell Emma just in the kitchen. Trinity looked to her left sharply. Night was asleep, that pain on his face still evident. Unable to speak, or barely breathe, Trinity shook Night roughly. His eyes darted open. They widened as he looked at Trinity, sitting up quickly.

"Tri—Trinity?" He knew it was her in front of him, but he couldn't believe it. Her eyes were large and glassy but sharp, evidence that her vision wasn't just human anymore. Night held her at the sides of her neck, gazing at her softly. She'd come back to him.

"You came back," he whispered. She nodded wildly, tears leaking from her eyes. She grabbed at her throat, trying to tell Night she couldn't talk or breathe.

"It's okay. Your body is still changing. Give it a moment and it will pass," he told her. She nodded, trusting his words. Just staring at him, those dark pools of comfort giving her complete ease. Little by little, her airway opened up, allowing for her to breathe. She clutched onto him as her gums throbbed. Using her tongue, she felt the tips of her teeth sharpen and elongate.

"Argh," she grunted, the pain making her close her eyes tight. Her stomach rolled with cramps, forcing her to bend forward.

"It hurts," her voice came out in a growl.

"You have to take my blood darling," Night told her. He bit into his own wrist to draw the first drop of blood. Trinity inhaled deeply, the tangy smell of his blood taking over her entire being. She snatched his arm and latched her mouth around his wrist, pulling hungrily at his blood. His vein opened up beautifully for her. When the blood hit her stomach, the cramps began to ebb, her hunger being satiated. She looked up at Night, their gazes locking. Those intense dark eyes and the passion that clawed out of them towards Trinity made her shudder again.

She sipped from his vein until her body told her it was enough. She licked at the two holes in his wrist from her fangs just like he'd done plenty of times to her. She swiped her tongue across her teeth feeling her fangs. They were smaller than Night's but just as sharp.

"You're mine Trinity. Forever," Night said.

"Our bond is eternal." Something about his statement impacted her deeply. Almost too deeply. She lunged at him, falling into his arms as she kissed his lips feverishly. What would she have done in the afterlife without having Night's touch? Without ever speaking to him again?

She ripped at her clothes, her nails sharp points. Night was tugging at her jeans, kissing her back with desperation. Trinity mounted his hips and yanked down the front of his jeans, freeing his erection. He was thick and full, beading at his tip with excitement. Trinity centered him at her entrance and sunk herself down slowly but surely. His breath hitched when her tightness encompassed him. He couldn't believe that he had almost lost her completely. She grinded on top of him, her mouth open as her head fell back. Her tiny fangs were cute and dangerous in her mouth, enticing Night even more. He sat up and peppered her neck with kisses.

"I love you Trinity," he said, holding onto her hips, helping her ride him. She moved up and down, gasping as his tip pushed past her boundaries into the deepness of her pleasure spots.

"I love you to Night," she moaned, shaking as she began to orgasm. He groaned and he busted, his release bursting through her guts, filling her until she overflowed.

"Whoa." Night wrapped his arms around Trinity, the moment he heard the intrusion of another voice. Trinity turned her head to see both Emma and Blaze standing in the doorway of the bedroom.

"I thought you were dead and you're in here bouncing on dick," Emma said, a smile teasing her lips. Trinity chuckled. She smiled brightly. Emma gasped at the sight of two fangs in Trinity's mouth.

"Pretty cool, huh?" Trinity asked. She turned around and looked at Night who was trying to use his arms to hide her ass from sight.

"My Night in shining armor saved me," Trinity whispered. Night winked at her and kissed her mouth tenderly. A cool breeze wafted between them. Night felt cold lips press to his cheek before it dissipated, melting away like it never existed.

"She's moved on," Trinity said. Night inhaled and nodded.

"Then we'll move on too. Together." She took his hand and placed it against her heart as she placed her hand against his heart.

"Together," he smiled.

"TRENT! TRENT!" Rose scrambled back into the house. She

was supposed to check if Vickie had regained consciousness but what she uncovered was even more worrisome.

"What?" Trent asked.

"Trinity-"

"I told you already I have some people that's coming to help me get rid of her body. Stop worrying about everything! You're going to make it worse!" Trent snapped.

"She's gone! Her body! It's gone!" Rose exclaimed.

"Gone? What do you mean gone?"

"It's not there! Vickie is still there, but Trinity, her body is gone!" Trent rubbed his eyes and dropped down into a chair.

"What in the fuck?" he cursed knowing that things indeed had gotten worse.

"Look, if people ask, we say she ran away. Because she ran off I began to grieve and Tracee was the one who comforted me and we fell in love. That's the story we're going with and that's it. You hear me?" Trent asked. Rose nodded nervously, her body shaking with fear. She'd agreed to kill her daughter and it could all come back to haunt her.

"James!" Trent shouted for Trinity's father. When he arrived, Trent explained what he did to Rose and then the same to Tracee.

"We don't know how her body got out of here but if anyone comes asking, we don't know shit. She ran away. If she somehow survived and told people we poisoned her, we can deny it. You'll tell people she's been on medication for delusions. I have a doctor that can forge those prescriptions for proof. If we stick to this then nothing will happen to us. Besides, it's her word against ours. No one will believe that we tried to kill her. We're all in this together, so if one of us go down, we're all going the fuck down. Stand strong and stick to the story. Got it?!" Trent was firm with his demands as he detailed their plans. Truthfully, he was forcing his voice not to quiver. However it was that Trinity disappeared, it would come back to haunt all of them in one way or the other.

Chapter Nineteen

TRINITY STARED AT HERSELF IN THE VANITY MIRROR, HER hair wild and kinky all over her head. Night was down on club level working. He still insisted that Trinity needed to rest, but after a week of being turned, she felt completely fine. Her body was so aware, her mind was sharp, her senses were intense. Being a vampire made her realize just how much she was missing out on as a human. Not only that, but feeding from Night sparked the arousal in her loins and she was riding his dick every time she drank his blood, frenzied with horniness. Her orgasms were richer when her fangs pierced Night's skin. It would rock her to the core when his larger fangs dipped into her veins while his thick long dick thrusted deeply into her body, tearing her away from humanity in the bout of so much pleasure. Trinity wouldn't trade any of this for the world. Yet, when she looked at herself all she saw was the human woman who nearly died. The human woman who's mother and father watched her clawing for her last breath and did nothing. The human woman whose parents cared more for a check than another life.

"What's up Vampira," Emma smiled, entering the room Trinity was sharing with Night. The club had become their home and Night wasted no time making sure she was comfortable. The other vampire females, using Night's stash of cash had bought her endless amounts of new clothing and anything Trinity could want.

"Nothing, just thinking," Trinity shrugged.

"Thinking about what? I know that look on your face isn't a good one," Emma said. Trinity didn't answer her. Emma glared at her before gasping.

"Are you pregnant?!" Emma squealed.

"Shut up before Night hears you! And no! I'm not pregnant. At least I don't think so," Trinity said. She winked at Emma, and tried to hide her smile.

"So, then what are you thinking about?" Emma asked.

"Remember how I always wanted to cut my hair?" Trinity asked. Emma nodded.

"Think you can hook me up? I never cut it because my parents would have freaked out. They were barely letting me wear it as an afro. But now that I'm changed, now that I'm with Night, I can be whoever I want to be. And I've always wanted a tapered hair cut with short curls at the top. There's no reason why I can't have it now," Trinity said.

"You are absolutely right. Leave who you were in the past because you've got a whole new future to live." Emma came up behind her. She reached for the shears tucked away on the vanity that Night had bought for Trinity so she'd have her own beauty space.

"Think Night will like it?" Emma asked, massaging her hands through Trinity's hair. Trinity sighed and shrugged.

"I don't know." Trinity wasn't going to act like she didn't care about Night liking her new look. She would be awfully hurt if he didn't because this was what she wanted. But she wasn't going to hide who she was for anyone. Not again.

"Just cut it," Trinity ordered.

"Alright. I will."

"NIGHT!" Emma's voice rang out above the music in the club. Night was counting liquor bottles behind the bar, while Blaze took notes of every brand they had in stock.

"What's up?" he asked her.

"Trinity wants you," she said. Night stood abruptly.

"Is she alright? I don't feel anything is wrong," he said, jumping over the bar.

"Whoa, relax. She's fine. She just wants you," Emma shrugged.

"Oh. Sheesh female, you're going to give me a heart attack," Night sighed.

"My name is Emma, Night, I keep telling you about that female crap!" Emma laughed. Blaze hopped over the bar and scooped Emma up.

"I'll just take her out of your hair Night, since she's so bothersome," Blaze smirked. While he whisked Emma away, Night headed in the opposite direction, going to the second floor where his heart was waiting.

The bedroom was dark when Night entered, but he knew Trinity wasn't asleep, he could feel her heart beating lively in a way that didn't represent sleep. She was nervous.

"What are you doing?" Night asked, knowing his heart was mischievous and always up to no good. In just a week, he'd never laughed so much and loved so hard as he did in his whole lifetime. The lights slowly came on, stopping at the dim setting. Night's eyes were pulled to the strippers pole he'd set up in the room. Trinity had claimed he'd had his toys and she wanted hers. With her new agility as a vampire, she was always twirling and climbing that damn pole, antagonizing Night with her sexuality.

She was walking around the pole, holding onto it as Night watched her. She smiled slyly before hooking her leg around the pole and twirling, showing off the red panties she knew were his favorite. Her body was long and elegant as she danced around the pole. Once he took his eyes from her body, he realized her head wasn't full of coils anymore. Her hair was cut low, tapered perfectly, still long enough on the top to show her kinks. Her lips were painted gray, and her eyes were deep set and smoky. Giving the pole one final spin, she stood and looked at Night, smiling seductively. Seeing her tiny fangs made his blood start to heat.

"You're so quiet," she said, sauntering over to him. Night gulped, trying to keep his cool.

"I'm just—I'm just in awe," he said.

"You're the most beautiful woman in this world. And you're mine," he said, running his hand through her short hair.

"You're my sexy vampire mate," he added, grabbing her plush bottom. Trinity laughed.

"I thought you wouldn't like it," she admitted.

"I told you. You're beautiful and I would love anything about you. I'd never force you to be something you're not," he said.

"Baby, how would I know if I'm pregnant?" Trinity asked him. Night was taken by surprise at her question. He took her wrist and bit into it softly, just enough to draw a tiny bit of blood. He swiped his tongue against the dribble of blood, savoring her taste. His eyes sparked amber as he looked at her. He tasted the hormones inside of her blood that changed the way she tasted.

"Did you—did you have a feeling?" Night asked her.

"I've felt...different. I didn't want to say anything to Emma until I knew for sure. When I drink your blood, I feel like I'm drinking more than I need to, like I'm really hungry. Then with the whole mating frenzy I went through after the change, I figured it only made sense. You were filling me up so much I felt like a banana cream donut," she chuckled. Night wrapped his arms around her. He inhaled deeply, his nose at her neck. Her scent had changed slightly as well but her pregnancy was too early for anyone to scent it if they weren't as close to her as Night was. And Night wasn't letting anyone close to his mate like that.

"But then I've only been a vampire a week. I didn't think I could get pregnant. with ovulating and all that stuff," Trinity added.

"Vampire females don't experience those kinds of effects. There's not ovulating and whatnot. Pregnancies just happen as long as both partners are vampires," Night explained. He inhaled her scent at her neck again.

"I can smell our baby. It smells like honeydew. Can't tell if it's a boy or girl though."

"How long will my pregnancy last?" Trinity asked.

"18 months," he shrugged. Trinity gasped.

"18 months?! Are you fucking kidding me?!" She screeched. Night burst out laughing. Trinity realized he was truly only joking with her. She hit him playfully.

"That's not funny!" she giggled.

"9 months darling. Just like if you were human."

"Well that's better." She wrapped her arms around his neck and held onto him tightly.

"I know where you're coming from Trinity, but I want you to know that you and my child will want for nothing. I'll love on you so much you'll probably try and run away," he said. Trinity threw her head back and laughed.

"You'll give me anything I want?" she asked.

"Anything Trinity," he vowed.

"There is one thing..." Trinity said softly.

Chapter Twenty

"TRENT! DID YOU HEAR THAT?!" TRACEE WAS AWOKEN from her slumber by the crashing of glass on the first floor. Trent slowly rose up, rubbing his eyes.

"Tracee, it's nothing. Probably Vickie dropped something. Let's go back to sleep baby," Trent tried to make Tracee lay back down but the unmistakable sound of footsteps made him halt. They were heavy foot falls. Too heavy to be Vickie. And there were more than one.

"Someone's in the house," Trent whispered. How'd they managed to break in, Trent had no idea. He'd had this place bunkered down tight.

Slipping out of bed, Trent grabbed for his pistol from his night table drawer. Tracee followed him out of the room, clutching his t-shirt. Trent moved slowly down the grand staircase. There was glass spilled in the foyer from the broken window. Carefully stepping over it, Trent walked towards the parlor that was still pitch black. The moment he stepped through the threshold; the lights flicked on. Trent felt his heart seize.

"What's the matter Trent? Looks like you've seen a ghost," Trinity grinned, biting into an apple she took from his fruit bowl. Her hair was cut beautifully and there was a glow to her skin, even in the dark jeans and t-shirt she wore.

"You—how—how are you here?" Trent quivered. His eyes moved to the two large men standing at her side. They were brooding, their arms crossed as they stared at Trent. Trinity stood and sauntered over to him.

"Well, I just walked in through the front door," she shrugged. "But I broke the glass so you'd wake up." She looked behind him and saw Tracee shivering behind him.

"Oh, so you really did hook up with my sister. You were for real about that. I just thought it was all part of that plan you had to kill me," Trinity said.

"You—you can't be here Trinity. Leave. Or I'll—"

"Or you'll what?!" Trinity snapped, cutting him off. She curled her lips back. Trent gasped and fell back when he saw the fangs popping from her gums. Trinity stuffed her half-eaten apple into his mouth and bitch slapped him. He fell to the ground, bringing Tracee with him.

"That's for slapping me," she spat at him. "I'd do much more to you, but my mate told me I couldn't. Not in my current state," she said.

"Ma—mate?" Trent blubbered. The large man with the locks stepped forward. Unlike Trinity's; his fangs were large and long.

"That's what she said. I'm the muthafucker she chose over you that made you so jealous you wanted to kill her. I don't know about you, but my woman is a precious thing. I wouldn't dare let her hands get dirty in this situation. But anything she wants; I shall give it to her. And she wants you dead."

"Please no!" Tracee shouted.

"No?! You fucking sat there and watched them poison me! Fuck that! if not for Night loving me I would be dead! And what? You'd be here living your best fucking life when all I wanted was to live my best life? If you'd just have let me go the both of us could have been happy. But no. Now, you can go to hell!" Trinity spat.

"You—you can't kill us! You're a vampire! It's against the law!" Trent exclaimed. Trinity grinned proudly.

"We're not going to kill you," she said.

"The jimsonweed you used to poison me is what's going to kill you," Trinity added. She motioned to the two teacups sitting on the small table.

"If you think I'm going to drink that, you've got another thing coming!" Trent objected.

"Oh, we know you're not going to drink it...willingly," Trinity smiled. Night barred his teeth as he lunged at Trent. He yanked Trent against his body and pried his mouth open. Trent fought and screamed, but the strength of a vampire outweighed him by far. Night ripped opened Trent's mouth. Blaze brought the teacup over and poured it's contents directly down Trent's throat. Night still held onto Trent, closing his mouth to make sure Trent swallowed the liquid and didn't try to spit it back up. Once it was swallowed, Night let Trent go and watched as he coughed and tried to vomit. Night looked at Tracee who was trying to crawl backwards.

"No," she begged. Trinity looked down at her sister for a moment. She tried to find one sense of sympathy and there was just none. Trinity reached out for the teacup. Blaze handed her the second one.

"What do you want to do Tracee? Drink it, or have it forced down your throat?" Trinity asked her sister softly. Tracee's eyes widened, realizing Trinity wasn't going to spare her.

"You were always such a bitch. Complaining and breaking rules and what? Now you're a murderer?" Trinity hummed.

"No Tracee. I'm just a vampire," Trinity shrugged. She balled her fist up and punched Tracee square in the face, the strength she'd acquired as a vampire nearly knocking Tracee clean out. As she tried to retain consciousness, Trinity forced

Tracee's mouth open and poured the tea down her throat, forcing her to drink the poison. Trinity squeezed her cheeks together until all the liquid was gone, then she slammed Tracee's head to the ground.

"Darling, I told you, if you get riled up it would pull at the savageness inside of you and our baby will be in danger. Come here," Night ordered softly. Trinity walked away from her sister and approached her mate. Night rubbed her neck and kissed her forehead, soothing her. She took several deep breaths, trying to fight her blood lust before it took over.

"Do you need to feed?" he asked her. With her pregnancy, she fed almost twice as normal.

"No. I'm okay," Trinity whispered.

"You better be okay. That's my niece or nephew in there," Blaze grumbled, crossing his arms. Trinity rolled her eyes at him but she couldn't help but smile.

A fit of coughing sounded behind them, Trent first and then Tracee, both of them trying to stand.

"You're going to rot in hell," Trent coughed out at Trinity.

"I don't see how. You're the one dying. Not me," Trinity shrugged. Trent's coughs became uncontrollable as he rolled around on the ground. His body began to seize as foam bubbled out of his mouth. His eyes went to the back of his head as the seizing of his body slowed until it finally stopped. Tracee soon followed. She rolled onto her stomach and went still, the poison taking its final effects.

"They're hearts have stopped," Trinity said, listening for the beat. A sharp gasp came from behind them. Vickie stood in the kitchen doorway, looking out at them. In a second, Blaze was behind her so she couldn't run off. Vickie was startled by the fast movement, but she didn't attempt to run.

"Same thing with this one?" Blaze asked.

"No. No. She was the only one who tried to come to my

rescue. That's why she was knocked out next to me in the garage. But what are you doing here Vickie?" Trinity asked.

"They all pretend you don't exist. I've been here. Collecting evidence, trying to make them pay. I have recordings of Trent planning things with your father. I was going to turn it over to the police. I thought—I thought you were dead."

"No, Vickie. I've become something else." She showed Vickie her fangs.

"Get away from here Vickie. There's nothing for you here anymore," Trinity told her.

"I—I called Charles. The day after they told me you were dead. I called him right up because I remembered you telling me to live my life. Charles was happy as ever to hear from me. He's been helping me with evidence and talking to the police. I intend to go and live with him once this is over," Vickie informed her. Trinity approached her and took her hands.

"I'm so happy for you Vickie. And trust me, it's over now. Trent is done for. Go be with Charles and forget this mess." Vickie nodded hastily. She hugged Trinity tightly.

"Be happy child," Vickie whispered to her. She looked at Night and nodded. Blaze moved out of her way, allowing Vickie to rush through the kitchen and leave out the back door.

Trinity sighed, feeling fatigued. She was barely pregnant and already tired. Hunger began to pan through her stomach, both for blood and for sticky sweet lemon cake and sweet tea.

"I feel your hunger darling. We should go and get this over with," Night warned. Trinity nodded and took his hand. Because she was a new vampire, her abilities for moving quickly and teleporting hadn't fully developed so she had to move with Night. Once he took her hand, they teleported out of Trent's home, leaving both the bodies of Trent and Tracee behind.

"HI DADDY," Trinity whispered. James woke up from his slumber, breathing heavily. His eyes widened, seeing Trinity sitting next to him on the bed.

"How—how is this—" he couldn't even speak.

"It's okay daddy. You don't have to worry about it," Trinity said. She smiled at him, her fangs still out for show.

"Rose wake up!" Her mother slowly woke. She turned around, seeing her daughter sitting on the edge of their bed. Her mouth fell. Trinity was stirring liquid in a teacup. She gave one cup to her father, and passed the second cup to her mother.

"Come now, drink up. You two love tea," Trinity said.

"Listen. Trinity about what happened-"

"No daddy. You listen. You wanted your money and your investment protected. I meant nothing to you. So much so that you allowed a man to orchestrate my death and you and mother just watched. That's okay. I've come to terms with the fact that you don't love me as your daughter. But not to worry. I have a mate now, a brother, and even Emma who loves me more than anything. I don't need you. So. Let's have a toast. Drink your tea."

"Trinity, this is just Ludacris! Did you do something to this tea?" her mother squeaked. Trinity took a deep breath and sighed.

"I just want to have tea with my parents. Isn't that what we always do?" Trinity asked.

"But—but you went missing after—and now you're a vampire—and-" Trinity groaned loudly.

"Alright, I'm tryna be fucking nice but it's like it's not working. I'm pregnant, getting tired, and I'm fucking starving. I don't have time for this shit. Drink the fucking tea!" Trinity snarled, showing her fangs.

"Drink the tea, and I leave!" Her father lifted the teacup with shaky hands. He took a small sip but it wasn't enough for her. Trinity pushed the cup against his face, forcing him to gulp down more. She gave her mother a cold stare and that was enough to get her mother to drink the tea.

"See, isn't that nice?" Trinity asked.

"You—you're pregnant?" Rose asked.

"Oh yeah." Trinity smiled.

"Maybe—maybe we can start over. If you let us, we'll be true grandparents." Trinity threw her head back and laughed.

"You must be out of your rabid ass mind," Trinity laughed.

"You think I'd ever let you anywhere near my baby? And my mate would not let you near his baby whatsoever, even if I begged," Trinity said.

"Never would I ever permit you near my child," Night conformed.

"Besides, did you really think I came here to just sip tea and talk?" Trinity asked. Her father began to cough first. The eyes of her parents widened in fear.

"You damn right, I poisoned your ass. So, even if I wanted to entertain your crazy ass idea about being grandparents, you won't even live long enough to see me poop while I give birth," Trinity shrugged. Rose began coughing, covering her mouth to try and hold herself back from coughing.

"Daddy, did you know that mother goes to a vampire club to get fucked?" Trinity asked politely. James gasped and looked at his wife, his throat beginning to constrict.

"How—how could you do that?" he croaked.

"I never forgave you for fucking my sister," she coughed.

"That was 20 years ago!"

"I don't care!" Rose shouted, a vicious cough tearing through her. Trinity stood from the bed and watched as her parents bickered back and forth. She shook her head. They were dying, yet arguing about stupid shit. They both took their last breaths with angered expressions and mouths that were foamed over.

"Take a good look Night," Trinity said.

"I'm looking Darling," he replied.

"If you ever fuck around on me, this will be your future." She walked away then, leaving her parents bedroom, refusing to look back at the bodies of the people who should have meant something to her.

"That's your mate," Blaze laughed, following Trinity out. Night was the last to leave. He caught up to Trinity and took her hand, teleporting her out of the home and outside of the gates.

He helped her onto his bike before he climbed on and revved up the engine. He sensed her hunger thriving deep inside of her and knew she needed to feed and have real food before she went ape shit.

"We're going home darling," Night assured her.

"Good. Because I can't wait to suck your blood and then suck everything else on your body," she whispered to him.

"Not if I suck your pussy clean first," he responded. A chill ran down her spine. Arousal and love sparked through the bond that thrived between them. He couldn't wait to spend eternity with her, just as much as she couldn't wait to spend eternity with him. Now, they had no reasons to look back on Trinity's past. They only had their future. Night revved the bike once more and took off, too eager to be sequestered with his beautifully pregnant mate.

The End...Maybe

For updates and more FOLLOW me on Social Media
IG: Authorjade_royal
FB: Author Jade Royal
Like Page:
@romanceauthor.jaderoyal
For exclusives and group discussions, JOIN MY READERS
GROUP!
https://www.facebook.com/groups/royalromantics/

CPSIA information can be obtained
at www.ICGtesting.com
Printed in the USA
LVHW040921181119
637663LV00006B/2628